THE
MONSTER
HYPOTHESIS

ROMILY BERNARD

Disney • HYPERION

LOS ANGELES   NEW YORK

First Edition, December 2019

10 9 8 7 6 5 4 3 2 1

FAC-020093-19298

Printed in the United States of America

This book is set in 11.5 point Palatino/Monotype and KG Fall For You/Fontspring.

Designed by Mary Claire Cruz

Library of Congress Cataloging-in-Publication Data
Names: Bernard, Romily, author.
Title: The monster hypothesis / by Romily Bernard.
Description: First edition. • Los Angeles ; New York : Disney Hyperion, 2019.
• Summary: While her famous-scientist parents are away, sixth-grader Kick Winter lives with her grandmother, a psychic, in Bohring, home to 453 people, 2,053 alligators, and one curse.
Identifiers: LCCN 2019002972 • ISBN 9781368028554 (hardcover)
Subjects: • CYAC: Middle schools—Fiction. • Schools—Fiction. • Psychics—Fiction. • Grandmothers—Fiction. • Blessing and cursing—Fiction.
Classification: LCC PZ7.B4551354 Mon 2019 • DDC [Fic]—dc23
LC record available at https://lccn.loc.gov/2019002972

Reinforced binding

Visit www.DisneyBooks.com

SUSTAINABLE FORESTRY INITIATIVE
Certified Sourcing
www.sfiprogram.org
SFI-00993
Logo Applies to Text Stock Only

For my mom, who knew Kick was amazing
from the very beginning

GRANDMA MISSOURI'S PREDICTION

"This will end badly."

It started with an explosion. Not a huge explosion, mind you, but one certainly large enough to send bits of floorboards everywhere. Some went down in flames. Some went up in smoke. The rest landed in Kick Winter's hair.

Not that she noticed.

"Should've reread those directions," she muttered, knowing full well that she hadn't read them in the first place.

Another bit of floorboard fizzled out, plunging into the ragged hole and sending the black cat, Butler, flying for cover. Kick coughed, waved smoke away from her face, and wondered if all burgeoning scientists had such unfortunate setbacks. She wasn't sure, and she chalked this one up to yet another example of school never teaching her anything she really needed to know.

Then again, setbacks might be the least of her problems,

because her grandmother was now standing in the kitchen doorway.

Kick's heart swung into her throat. For an old woman with a limp, Grandma Missouri could move *fast* when the situation warranted it.

Like right now, when her kitchen had acquired unexpected ventilation.

"Kick! Winter!" Grandma Missouri lurched forward, one hand white-knuckled around her cane.

"It was an accident!"

"An accident?"

"Absolutely!" Kick tried to laugh. It came out a sputter. "You know how these things go. You don't know you're having an accident until you're having one and—"

Crack!

Another piece of kitchen floor tipped into the still-smoking hole. Grandmother and granddaughter listened to it land with a hearty *plop*. Fortunately for everyone, the Hollows—the tiny cottage where they lived—was built on stilts above the swamp, and the flaming bits simply fell into the murky water. Unfortunately for Figgis—the enormous alligator who lived under the Hollows—those flaming bits were now raining on him.

As Kick watched, Figgis floated past the hole, slimy with mud and looking distinctly put out.

Or maybe that was just how the alligator normally

looked. She wasn't sure. She'd only been at the Hollows for a few days.

"Your aunt was right," Grandma Missouri said at last, studying the singed hole with wide eyes. She sat down heavily on a kitchen chair, the tiny bells on her skirt jingling. "You really are going to grow up to be an evil genius."

Kick sighed and dusted herself off. "I'm not going to be an evil genius. I'm going to be the world's greatest *scientist*. I'm going to help people just like my parents do—and science isn't evil." She paused as Figgis floated by again, eyeing her. He blew indignant bubbles. Or, they seemed indignant. Again, it was hard to tell with alligators. "At least, science isn't evil when it gets up in the morning, but sometimes explosions happen."

"What were you *thinking*?" Grandma Missouri demanded, clutching the lace collar of her dress. Kick's grandmother wasn't usually into lace—or bells for that matter—but Mr. Jessup was coming by later to have his cards read, and he thought all psychics should look like the ones on television.

For the record, they did not. Grandma Missouri usually dressed like an old Hollywood starlet with careful curls and elbow-length gloves, but she said a customer who came twice a week *every* week didn't need to be understood, just accommodated.

"I don't know what I was thinking." Kick flipped to a new page in her experiment book and scribbled:

Friday, September 6
Think about reading directions.

She set her pen down. "Maybe we should call Mom and Dad."

"We are not calling your parents. Georgia's working."

Kick frowned. It was true. Georgia was Grandma Missouri's daughter and Kick's mother, but to the rest of the world, she was Dr. Georgia Winter, super scientist. She traveled a lot, making the world better, and sometimes she was so busy making the world better, she had to leave Kick behind. Sometimes it was for a few days. Sometimes it was . . . longer.

And this time might very well be the longest yet.

Kick chased away the thought. She had to. If she let it linger, her brain would turn against her. It would think about how she was losing her parents in pieces: Her mother's perfume had already faded from her clothes. Would the feel of her father's hand holding her own be next? It seemed possible. Chemicals weren't the only things that evaporated.

"Your mother has enough worries without us adding to them." Grandma Missouri patted her granddaughter's shoulder. "We can handle this ourselves. We have each other."

"True."

"And besides, we don't want to ruin this for you. Staying here is a reward."

This was also true. It *would* be a reward for most children to stay with their grandmother, but that was because most children's grandmothers were soft and sweet and liked to bake. Their grandmothers were not town psychics—and they definitely were not *fake* town psychics. Which, in this case, meant Grandma Missouri took people's money and told them what they wanted to hear.

"There are worse jobs," Grandma Missouri would tell Kick whenever she asked about it.

"Like what?" Kick would want to know.

"I'll tell you later. Now help an old lady with her wind machine."

And Kick would help because Grandma Missouri *was* old, but also because it was important to properly hide a fake psychic's wind machine, otherwise everyone would know she was a fake and that wasn't good for business.

"Kick?"

She turned. Her grandmother still sat at the chipped kitchen table, shoulders slumped like an old pillow. "Yes?"

"Who gave you that chemistry set? Your father?"

Kick paused. She was pretty sure this was what Grandma Missouri called a "loaded question." She was also pretty sure her grandmother already knew the answer and wasn't happy about it. Grandma Missouri and James Winter didn't like each other much.

"It's to continue my exploration into the fields of science." Something popped and plopped into the water below. "I'm supposed to record my theories and proposed experiments."

Grandma Missouri nodded. "Remind me to get your father an ant farm for a welcome-home present."

"But the ants always get out of those things and—" *And that's the point*, Kick realized. *Time for a distraction.*

But with what? She glanced around the kitchen for inspiration. Through the windows over the sink, she could see swamp trees rising up like gnarled fingers, crusty with moss and scabby with ivy. Through the hole, she could see Figgis.

"Maybe you could tell Mr. Jessup an angry spirit did it," she said at last.

Grandma Missouri thought it over, attention still on her ruined floor or maybe on Figgis. As they watched, a bumblebee drifted up through the smoke and wandered toward one of the kitchen's wide windows. "Or *maybe*," her grandmother said, "I'll tell him the curse is upon us, and he better bring his grandkids in for preventative blessings."

Kick rolled her eyes. Ever since she'd arrived, the Bohring Town Curse was all anyone could talk about. According to legend, every hundred years all the Bohring children turned into monsters and took over the town. Kick couldn't get a clear answer as to why, though. Grandma

Missouri said it was just the way curses worked. Mr. Jessup said it was because the Bohring town swamp was magical, and he said it with such conviction chills had climbed up the back of Kick's neck. It almost felt *true*.

Almost.

Then Kick remembered Mr. Jessup once searched for a gas leak with a lit match—his eyebrows still hadn't fully grown back—so clearly his judgment was suspect. She took a deep breath, counted to ten for patience, and when that didn't work, she counted to twenty.

"There's no such thing as curses," she told her grandmother.

"You don't call this *monstrous*?"

Technically, Kick would call it the unfortunate combination of potassium nitrate and sulfur, but she was wise enough not to say so. "There's no such thing as monsters."

"The world is *full* of monsters."

"There's no such thing—"

"There is such a thing as being grounded. No more experiments." Grandma Missouri leaned forward so their noses almost brushed. Kick narrowed her eyes into slits. The two glared at each other. "Don't think this will make me change my mind about keeping you," Grandma Missouri said, hoisting herself to her feet and trading her cane for a yellow-handled broom. "First, we're going to tidy up."

Kick looked from the smoldering hole in the floor to

the charred cabinet baseboards to the spool of fishing line still sitting on the countertop because Grandma Missouri needed to install it in the séance room. Tidy up? She wondered if the fumes had overcome her grandmother.

For the record, Kick shouldn't have wondered. Grandma Missouri was intimidated by nothing—not holes in floors, not suspicious clients looking for fishing line that might suspend tablecloths at opportune moments, not *even* deep-frying candy bars. In fact, Kick had once watched her grandmother deep-fry a stick of butter.

A *stick*. Of *butter*.

But Kick didn't have time to consider any of this because Grandma Missouri passed her a dish towel.

"After we finish cleaning," her grandmother added, sweeping bits of glass beakers into a pile, "we're going into town to register you for school. Clearly, you need to be kept busy."

Busy? In a town named Bohring? *Highly unlikely,* Kick thought, but again, she was wise enough not to say so. She picked up her chemistry book and what was left of her evaporating dish and—she frowned. The evaporating dish wouldn't budge. It was stuck to the Formica countertop.

"Definitely need to be kept busy," Grandma Missouri said to herself, sweeping faster. "This is exactly what I've been telling Georgia. People need *roots,* a *home,* and I have never in all my life met a child more in need of *friends.*"

"I'm not lonely," Kick said quickly. And she wasn't. She'd been *left*—but only because her parents had gone abroad to help grow crops for at-risk population. Yes, she missed doing experiments with her father on the weekends and cooking with her mother in the evenings, and yes, it sort of felt the same as being lonely and looked the same as being lonely, but it wasn't. Kick was positive.

"I'm not lonely," she repeated.

Her grandmother ignored her. "Nope," she continued, sweeping the last of the glass into the pile and the pile into the hole. Figgis thrashed his tail. "The child needs Bohring, and she's staying in Bohring."

Kick sighed again, and this time, she made sure to sound especially long-suffering. It wasn't hard. After all, if Grandma Missouri were *really* worried about her grand-daughter becoming an evil genius, she would've realized staying in Bohring—human population 453, alligator population 2,053, mosquito population innumerable—was actually an excellent way to turn her into one.

There was nothing to do.

There was nothing interesting going on.

But as usual, only Kick noticed these things.

GRANDMA MISSOURI'S PREDICTION

"Things are about to get worse for you."

The clock struck three when a grim-faced Grandma Missouri and a slightly singed Kick walked through the front doors of Bohring Elementary and Middle School. Kick's last school had smelled like mold and floor polish, but this one smelled like new paint and newer tennis shoes. It was bright and shiny with dark brick on the outside and creamy-colored walls on the inside. There were student pictures in the hallways and trophy cases by the windows, and Kick—who understood the importance of ambience better than most people—decided she would give the school an A-plus for presentation.

Even if it *was* a little empty.

"Where is everyone?" Kick asked.

"Most children like to play outside."

"Funny."

"I know." Grandma Missouri smiled, but she didn't smile for long because the blond woman standing behind the giant reception desk gave her a stack of paperwork to fill out. Kick's grandmother wasn't big on forms. They made her nose wrinkle like she was smelling burned kitchen floorboards. "Are you sure you need *all* of these?" she asked, flipping through the forms.

"Quite sure."

Grandma Missouri glared at the receptionist. The receptionist glared back. She was a narrow woman with sunburned cheeks and ghostly-pale hands. She should've seemed small next to Grandma Missouri's voluminous dress and generous figure. Instead she looked . . . sharp.

"I don't think we've met." Grandma Missouri heaved her massive red purse onto the counter, and something inside of it squeaked. "I'm Missouri Jackson."

The receptionist blinked.

"Missouri Jackson. The psychic."

Another blink.

Heat began to roll up Kick's neck. *Can someone self-combust from embarrassment?* she wondered. At the moment, it seemed likely.

The receptionist cocked her head. Her blond hair was slicked back into a tight bun and it glinted under the overhead light. "Well, I'm Dr. Malinda Callahan. The school psychologist."

"Psychologist?" Grandma Missouri's purse squeaked again and she thumped it. "Psychology is for hippies, dear. Are you sure you're fulfilling your destiny? I sense something far more . . . organic about you. And when did we need a psychologist for paperwork? What happened to Bessy?"

"Shouldn't you know?"

"Your aura is overwhelming me. It's very green."

The corner of Dr. Callahan's left eye twitched. "Bessy's out sick and we're short-staffed, so I'm helping."

Grandma Missouri nodded as if she had expected nothing less. "And yet I suspect the universe wants more for you."

"Considering I hold dual doctorates in biology and psychology, I'm fairly certain 'the universe' is perfectly happy with me."

"Is it?" Grandma Missouri's voice tilted up, and Kick winced. A prediction was coming. "Because daughters of Bohring—especially daughters of Bohring who go on to such magnificent accomplishments—don't usually return to, uh, fill in."

As if on cue, Dr. Callahan's nostrils flared with indignation.

Kick grimaced. In the last four years, her parents had worked in six different cities, which meant Kick had gone to six different schools, and thanks to those six different cities and schools, she knew all about being the New Girl, the New Smart Girl, and especially the New Smart Girl Who Has No Friends and Sits Alone at Lunch.

But she'd never been the New Smart Girl the School Staff Hates. Thanks to Grandma Missouri, that seemed likely to change.

Grandma Missouri shrugged. "Well, *we* might be strangers, but I'm sure you know my other granddaughter? Carolina?"

"Oh!" Dr. Callahan leaned across the desk to look down at Kick, then looked up at Grandma Missouri. She seemed to be making a decision. Kick prayed it was to refuse enrollment.

Pleasepleaseplease, she thought. The only thing worse than being the New Girl again would be getting into school because of her cousin.

"*Everyone* knows Carolina," Dr. Callahan said at last. "Such a gifted child—and *such* a huge vocabulary."

Kick rolled her eyes. Some of that vocabulary was because Carolina's mother was a lawyer and her father was a retired super scientist. The rest was because Carolina was a know-it-all.

Dr. Callahan studied her clipboard for several seconds, pale fingers playing with the magnolia-shaped pendant around her neck. "Let me see what I can do, Miss Missouri."

"Thank you," Grandma Missouri said, waiting until the psychologist had stepped away before leaning down to Kick. "Did you hear the way she talked about your cousin?"

Kick rolled her eyes again. Of course she heard the way

Dr. Callahan talked about her cousin. Adults *always* said Carolina's name with joy and reverence. It would be annoying if Kick were bothered by such things. Luckily, she wasn't.

Much.

"You're going to get in today," her grandmother added. "I will bet you my famous swamp cake *I* don't have to do the paperwork."

"I don't want to bet against you."

"Why not?"

"Because you always win."

Grandma Missouri grinned. "That's because I can read people." She straightened, smoothing her delicate leather driving gloves. They were supposed to make her look elegant—and they did—but Kick suspected her grandmother really liked them because they made her feel like a European race-car driver. "How do you think I knew Dr. Callahan was a former Bohring resident?"

"No idea, but I'm pretty sure you're going to tell me."

"Peeked in her Prius as we drove in. Though she may have been gone long enough to think that little car is suitable for dirt roads and swamp flooding, she hasn't forgotten she'll need her snake-proof boots for when she goes hiking. Fang Proof Boots are only sold at the Grimp and Myer, so she had to be a local. And *how* did I know she was a gardener?"

For a beat, Kick had no idea, and then suddenly she did. "The sunburn, the necklace, and the pale hands. She's out in the sun a lot, but she must wear gloves." She paused. "'Green' and 'organic' were nice touches."

"I know. You can tell everything you need to know by reading a person. That's how you'll make your fortune, dear girl."

"I don't want to trick people. I want to be a scientist."

Grandma Missouri blew out an exasperated breath. "Listen here, Miss Smarty-Pants, people don't mind being tricked into feeling smart nearly as much as they mind being talked to like they're stupid. You would do well to remember that."

Kick opened her mouth, but Dr. Callahan and her clipboard returned. "Miss Missouri," she said, "since these are special circumstances, we'll make an exception for the paperwork. You can turn it in later."

"I do appreciate that." Grandma Missouri shouldered her red purse. It squeaked again. Kick and Dr. Callahan both eyed the purse, and Grandma Missouri pretended not to notice. "Kick's living with me at the Hollows until her parents return."

Dr. Callahan paled. Kick smiled. The new school psychologist might not recognize her grandma, but around here, the Hollows' reputation preceded it.

"She's living out there?" Dr. Callahan asked the question in the same tone someone would ask, *You eat children?* or *You never brush your teeth?*

Kick understood the tone. In fact, she understood it better than almost anyone because she was indeed living at the Hollows. And it was indeed horrifying.

But it was only horrifying if you didn't know the black cat, Butler, purred like a tiny outboard motor. Or if you didn't know the overgrown grass smelled sweet at night. It was especially horrifying if you didn't know Figgis was more interested in eating expired chicken cutlets from Winn-Dixie than he was in eating children.

Dr. Callahan didn't know any of that, though, and if Kick told her, Grandma Missouri would skin Kick alive for ruining the Hollows' terrifying reputation.

"Of course she's living at the Hollows. Where else would she live?" Grandma Missouri waited for an answer and Dr. Callahan went back to her clipboard.

"And her name is Karis?" she asked, peeking up at Kick.

Kick lifted her chin. "No. My name is Kick."

Dr. Callahan looked at her grandmother. "Is that really what you want her to be called?"

Grandma Missouri shrugged. "If that's what the child wants to be called."

"Interesting." Dr. Callahan wrote something down on her clipboard, looking very, well, psychologisty. She pulled off a piece of paper and handed it to Kick, exposing the white line of her wrist. "Your new schedule."

"Thank you," Kick said, holding her breath as she

scanned the columns. She had reading, math, social stud-
ies, gym, and . . . natural science. "Dr. Callahan?"

"Yes?"

She placed the schedule on the desk and slid it toward
her. "There aren't any real science classes on my schedule."

"That's not true." The psychologist smiled like Kick
was especially stupid. "There's *natural* science. Right there.
You're going to get to build a volcano!"

"The predictable response of sodium bicarbonate and
acetic acid is perfectly fine," Kick said. *If you like being bored
to death,* she thought. "But I'd like to sign up for chemistry,
please. Or any other class where students work with real
acids."

Kick didn't think any other classes would work with
real acids, but she thought it was important to appear
open-minded.

Dr. Callahan gaped and gaped, and finally: "We would
never let you work with real acids! That's terrible!"

"It's only terrible if you spill them." Kick was trying for
polite, but it was definitely a strain.

"Ha. Ha. Kick." Grandma Missouri's laugh was forced.
She shifted her red purse to her other shoulder, and this time,
it didn't squeak. Kick wasn't sure if she should be relieved
or worried. "Why ever would you ask such a thing?"

Kick stared at her grandmother. If Grandma Missouri
didn't know why Kick would ask about chemistry, then

she really hadn't been paying much attention for the past eleven years.

Or paying much attention this morning.

"Because," Kick explained, "in chemistry, you take stuff and put it together with other stuff and come up with something else entirely." She paused, waiting for the adults to nod with understanding, and when they didn't, she shrugged. "I like seeing what I can do."

Grandma Missouri blinked, and then looked at Dr. Callahan. "Aren't children funny?"

"Hilarious," Dr. Callahan said, but she didn't mean it. Kick could tell. She was pretty sure Grandma Missouri could tell too. "You'll take natural science like the rest of the children," she said with a sniff. *"Chemistry.* Why, I *never."*

Kick could well imagine that Dr. Callahan never did. In fact, Kick figured there were a *lot* of things Dr. Callahan never did.

But luckily for everyone, she didn't get a chance to say it because the attendance office's door opened. Afternoon sunlight caught the newcomers from behind, stretching three shadows across the wide reception desk.

And Kick—who didn't believe in magic or spirits or premonitions—shivered.

"Your troubles will come in a pack of three."

Dr. Callahan turned. Kick could hear the smile in her voice when she said, "Oh, hello, ladies!"

"Hi, Dr. Callahan!" The three girls had shiny white smiles and matching green dresses, and when they walked toward the reception desk, they walked in unison.

"Ladies," Dr. Callahan said, "this is Kick Winter. She's new here, so introduce yourselves."

"I'm Jenna B.," said the first girl.

"I'm Jenna H.," said the second girl.

"And I'm"—the third girl pushed ahead of the other two—"Jenna Jane."

Every school Kick had ever attended had girls like the Jennas. They might be named Ella or Lacey or Anita, but they were always the same and Kick could always spot them. They dressed alike. They talked alike. They were only friends with each other.

Although sometimes they weren't very friendly to each other at all.

Bottom line, the Jennas of the world were like the sun and everyone revolved around them. If they liked you, *everyone* liked you, and one day, Kick was going to study them. She was going to figure out if it was something in their bubble gum that made them Jennas.

Or if it was something else altogether.

And even though the girls kind of, sort of terrified Kick, her heart also kind of, sort of leaped at the sight of them. They smiled at her like they wanted to be . . . friends.

Not that I'm lonely, Kick thought, and she thought it over and over until it felt true.

"I'll be with you in a moment," Dr. Callahan told the Jennas before turning back to Kick and Grandma Missouri. "Your teacher is Mrs. Flagg. She's in room six. Down that hallway."

Kick turned, looking in the direction Dr. Callahan was pointing. There were only two hallways, and Kick's class was apparently down the left-hand one.

"School is the greatest time of your life," the psychologist added, turning her voice extra deep and somber. It reminded Kick of when Grandma Missouri was pretending to be a spirit speaking from the beyond. It didn't impress Kick then either.

"Enjoy every minute—it also starts at eight thirty sharp

on Monday." Dr. Callahan tapped her clipboard against the desktop before turning to the Jennas. "Ladies? Do you think you could show Miss Kick around our fine school? She'll need to know where everything is."

The Jennas all nodded, ponytails bouncing. "We'd be happy to," Jenna Jane said, and Kick's heart jumped. Twice.

Jenna Jane turned to Kick. "Ready?"

"Um . . . okay."

"Are you sure?" Grandma Missouri whispered, and for a grandma who had very recently been muttering about how Kick needed friends, she seemed a touch nervous. She cut her eyes to the Jennas as she tied her white silk scarf over her Joan Crawford–esque curls. Grandma Missouri might like to drive fast, but she did it in style. "Because if you're not sure, you could come home with me."

"I'm sure."

"Will you remember how to get home?"

Kick nodded. There was only one road out of Bohring, and as long as she kept following it, she'd reach the Hollows. It wasn't much over a mile away.

Mostly because nothing was much over a mile away in Bohring.

Not the hardware store, which was owned by the mayor and had a decidedly disappointing selection of solvents. Not the Curl Up and Dye beauty parlor, which was right next door and always smelled like ammonia and cigarettes.

And certainly not the Grimp and Myer convenience store, which sold bait and tackle, canned goods, and the occasional taxidermied squirrel to Grandma Missouri.

Grandma Missouri leaned close. "Mr. Jessup's coming at four. I have to get . . . *ready.*"

Kick nodded again. In this case, "ready" meant her grandmother had to check the Spirit Communicator for optimal table shaking and double-check that the fishing line couldn't be seen. Most people didn't require either for a card reading, but as mentioned before, Mr. Jessup had certain expectations about psychic experiences, and he preferred his spirits to be fully functional.

"I'll be fine." And she would be. The Jennas seemed nice enough.

But a teeny tiny part of her hoped it might be the start of something more.

***

Later that night, when Kick looked back on this moment, she decided to blame her mother for what happened. Generally speaking, mothers are quite useful like that. You can blame them for all sorts of things, but in this case it was particularly true.

You see, Dr. Georgia Winter believed life was filled with Important Moments, and she was always telling Kick to look out for them. Sometimes, Important Moments were opportunities. Sometimes, they were Turning Points.

And sometimes, they were truly Unfortunate Setbacks.

"Bottom line," Georgia would always say, "Important Moments are the moments in your life where something is about to change. Everyone's Important Moments are different, though, so you have to learn to recognize them. Thankfully, our family's really good at it, so you will be too."

Kick hadn't been so sure. "How do you know? What if I'm *not* good at it?"

"But you are. You take opportunities and push for more—just like I do. But when I was young, people didn't just *laugh* at me when I said I wanted to be a scientist, they didn't *believe* I could *ever* do it. Remember, I was a girl, and we didn't have much money. When people think of future scientists do they think of those things?"

"No?" Kick had guessed, hoping she was wrong.

"No," her mother had said, "they think of people they already know like Einstein or Sagan or maybe Hawking, but not people like me—so I had to find my own Important Moments and take them."

Which meant Important Moments could change the course of your destiny—as long as you could identify them—and Kick was pretty sure she had properly identified this as an Important Moment. The Jennas were being friendly because they wanted to be friends.

Right?

They showed Kick the girls' bathroom, the library, the cafeteria, and, finally, her new classroom. Mrs. Flagg's door was the third on the right, and it was decorated with paintings of watercolored flowers and a laminated poster of a kitten hanging from a tree branch.

Kick peeked through the door's slender window and pretended she didn't notice how the Jennas were peeking at her. In later years, Kick would associate matching outfits with children in scary movies and, well, the Jennas, but right now she was only aware of their candy-colored dresses, and the grease spot on her coveralls.

"So that's it," Jenna Jane announced, flinging her arms wide and smiling like she'd won a television contest. "This is everything."

"It's nice," Kick told her. "Thank you for showing me around."

It was a very polite response, and it must have been the *right* response because Jenna Jane's smile deepened. It wrinkled up her eyes and dug two dimples into her cheeks before she asked, "So what kind of a name is 'Kick'?"

Considering how many times people asked that question, Kick knew she should have a ready-made answer, but she didn't. She did, however, know she was too tall and too skinny and liked science, and when one was too tall and too skinny and liked science, one could often end up stuffed into lockers or swirlied into toilets.

Kick liked to think her nickname made it seem unwise
for bullies to do either, and *that* was why she picked it.

But by now the silence had gone on for too long and the
Jennas were staring her down, gazes traveling from Kick's
sneakers to her coveralls to her face.

"It's my name," Kick said finally. "I like it."

The Jennas exchanged a look. It said, *This is stupid*, or
more likely, *This girl is weird*. Either way, Kick's armpits
went swampy.

"And that Missouri woman," Jenna Jane said slowly,
twisting the tip of her hair around and around her finger.
"She's really your grandmother?"

Kick nodded.

"Wow," Jenna Jane said. "You know, everyone in town
thinks your family is *so* special."

"Very special," Jenna B. echoed.

Jenna H. giggled. "Yah, Mom says it takes someone
really special to wear satin evening gowns during the day
like Miss Missouri wears."

"And scarves like Miss Missouri wears," Jenna Jane
added.

"And has a daughter who runs around the world looking for attention," Jenna B. said. They were circling her
now, so close Kick could smell their cherry bubble gum.
Before she'd thought they looked exactly alike, but now she
could see their differences: Jenna H. had freckles buried

under pale powder, Jenna B. had lip gloss on her teeth, and Jenna Jane had pale powder *and* lip gloss. But their eyes had the same gleam.

"And then there's Carolina," Jenna Jane added flatly, like that was all there was to say, and maybe that was true. She stood right in front of Kick. "Seems like your whole family's special."

Kick lifted her chin. "We *are*."

"Oh, yeah? What makes *you* so special?"

Kick considered this. She could say she was special because she knew so much science, that she was special because she had parents who knew even more, but none of that would impress the Jennas. In Kick's experience, Jennas and their variations were only ever impressed with pop stars, cute boys, and the truly amazing.

An idea bloomed just underneath her heart, like it had been waiting: It would be truly amazing if she said she was psychic.

Kick knew exactly how to do it too. She'd watched her grandmother for years.

But I couldn't, she thought, appalled with herself. *Could I?*

"Hel-*lo*? Are you deaf?" Jenna Jane asked, and Jenna H. and Jenna B. giggled.

"I'm special because I want to be a scientist," Kick said at last. It was the truth, and even though Grandma Missouri said the truth would set Kick free (and this was the truest thing Kick had said since arriving in Bohring), she didn't feel free at all. Standing under the Jennas' stares, she felt pasted to the floor.

Jenna H. snorted. "Good luck with that."

"Yah, seriously," Jenna B. added.

Jenna Jane just smiled, and that smile gave Kick chills.

"Girls?" Dr. Callahan's voice floated down the hallway, and all four girls turned. The school psychologist stood by the trophy case, arranging a flowered hat with one hand. Her handbag dangled off her other arm. "I need to lock up. Could you show Kick the playground?"

"Yes, Dr. Callahan!" the Jennas chorused.

"See you tomorrow!" Dr. Callahan waved.

"Yes, Dr. Callahan!" The Jennas' voices were singsong, but their expressions were flat.

They don't want to show me the playground, Kick realized, stomach sinking an inch—and then another. *Grandma Missouri is right. You* can *read people if you look closely enough.*

But she really wished she hadn't looked at all.

"You are about to embark on a new beginning."

Monday came all too quickly. Kick had always hated the first day of school—depressing, really, since she was pretty sure she had many, many more coming. Scientists were supposed to love learning, and Kick did. She *did*.

She just didn't necessarily enjoy the new schedule and the new students and how everybody always knew each other and she never knew any of them.

Well, technically, she knew the Jennas and Carolina, but that wasn't comforting.

At all.

"Kick?" Grandma Missouri thumped her cane against the staircase again. A picture of Figgis fell off the wall and onto Kick's bed. She stared at it. Even upside down, the alligator looked hungry. "You're going to be late!"

An interesting proposition, Kick thought until she realized being late would also mean coming into class after school had started. It was bad enough that she was starting two weeks after everyone else.

"Coming!" she bellowed, dragging herself out of bed and picking her coveralls off the floor. They smelled like Grandma Missouri's incense, like sandalwood and earth, and it made her nose itch. She wedged one foot and then the other into sneakers, and allowed herself two minutes to check her latest experiment: glow-in-the-dark slime.

It was congealing in her closet and turning out rather well. At least, Kick was pretty sure it was turning out rather well. She consulted her singed chemistry book once more, hoping she hadn't left anything out. Increasingly, it was difficult to read around the scorch marks.

Now, a lesser scientist might observe that glow-in-the-dark slime wasn't much of a step up from baking-soda volcanoes, but those lesser scientists never had to erect a backup chemistry set in their closet. Technically speaking— which coincidentally was the kind of speaking Kick preferred—she wasn't supposed to be experimenting with anything, let alone growing slime, but science waited for no one.

Hence the closet laboratory. In her future memoirs, Kick planned to discuss why a closet was not an ideal location for scientific advancements. There wasn't enough room, there definitely wasn't enough storage, and she was pretty sure her carpet was flammable.

She flipped off the overhead light, plunging the tiny closet into darkness, and watched her slime go supernatural green.

Nice, she thought, moving her Bunsen burner to the floor so she had room to write. Maybe there was some—well, *one*—thing good about a closet laboratory. Kick turned the light on and took her notebook off the dresser serving as her lab table and noted the day (Monday, September 9), the time (7:23 a.m.), and the slime's color (turning a bit vomit green). She closed the notebook and felt very official. When her parents came back, they could see all the experiments she'd completed and read her hypotheses for new experiments.

They would be so proud.

Satisfied with her slime, Kick tucked the notebook under one arm, turned off the overhead light again, and shut the closet door. Grandma Missouri had a bad knee and never came upstairs, but Kick shoved dirty clothes in front of her closet to be extra safe. She stood back, examining her handiwork.

"An absolute pigsty," she said, and smiling, bounced downstairs. Breakfast at the Hollows usually meant cheesy grits or honeyed oatmeal. It meant Grandma Missouri at the stove and a kitchen as humid as the yard.

Today, however, it meant cereal and circling around the hole in the floor.

Technically, the hole was covered. Grandma Missouri

had nailed a plywood square over it, but Kick still edged carefully around the repair. It would be just her luck to fall through and have to go to school smelling like swamp and Figgis.

She poured herself a bowl of wheaty squares, took a huge bite, and listened to her grandmother *clomp clomp clomp* through the séance room. Something was up. Grandma Missouri never had visitors this early and—

Bing! Biiinnnggg!

The doorbell! Kick's heart swung like a pendant on a chain. *Mom? Dad?* She leaped from the kitchen table and took off down the hallway.

Bing! Biiinnnggg! Kick ran faster. Faster.

Oops.

Her sneakers hit the rug, and she skidded. Her elbow smacked the wall. Her knee walloped Cecil, her grandmother's taxidermied bear, and Cecil's top hat fell off. Butler yowled, and Kick tumbled to the floor. For several seconds, she stared up at the dusty candelabra and wondered if she'd broken her butt. It *hurt*.

And her parents weren't there.

Kick brushed herself off as her cousin let herself inside. "Hey, Carolina."

Carolina nodded. "Hey, yourself. Blown up anything else?"

"It was *once*—and no." Usually, Kick would have had a

better response, but she was momentarily transfixed by her cousin's dress. Maybe more than momentarily. *That is a lot of fluff,* Kick thought.

And it was.

Carolina's puffy skirt made her wider than she was tall—which was really saying something because Carolina was as tall and thin as Kick. Her shirt was white and rib-boned, her socks were white and frilly, and her skirt was pink. But it was a violent pink, like angry cotton candy or a really bad case of poison oak.

It was, in other words, classic Aunt Aly. Kick's aunt had a stressful job being an important lawyer, and she dealt with that stress by dressing up Carolina.

Work must be hard right now, Kick thought.

Her cousin's eyes narrowed. "Looking at something?"

"A lot of somethings actually."

"Like I care what someone who wears overalls as a fashion choice thinks."

"They're *coveralls*, and they make getting dressed *fast*." They did too. Kick thought of her coveralls as her speed suit, but only to herself because no one else would understand.

"Are you two fighting already?" Grandma Missouri appeared in the hallway. Her hair was twisted around rollers, and she was rubbing some sort of cream into her cheeks. "One of these days, you're going to have to learn to get along."

Never going to happen, Kick thought, but she knew better than to argue. "What are you doing?" she asked her grandmother.

"Do you think all of this"—Grandma Missouri motioned from her fake-fur-trimmed dressing gown to her cream-covered cheeks to the rollers—"happens without a little help?"

"No?" Kick guessed to be polite, but she really, *really* hoped her grandmother wouldn't tell her.

Grandma Missouri knotted her robe a little tighter and motioned to an enormous white cardboard box on the floor. "Help me get my delivery in the séance room before you trip over it too."

Carolina stayed by the door, nose wrinkled. "Mom says I'm not to help you with your lies and distortions, Grandma Missouri."

"I'm not asking for help with *that.* I'm asking for help with my new crystal ball. It's heavy. What does your mother say about keeping an old lady from getting a herniated disk?"

"A herniated what?"

"Help me move my crystal ball," Grandma Missouri said. "Or I'll put the eye on you."

Carolina rushed to their grandmother's side. "That's better," Grandma Missouri said with a grunt. Together, the three of them wedged their fingers under the box and heaved. For a tiny cottage out in the swamp, the Hollows got a lot of packages. Sometimes, it was from the vintage clothing shop in Atlanta that sent Grandma Missouri her gorgeous clothes. Other times, it was from places like Itella Ur Fortune.

And this is one of those times, Kick thought, recognizing the address label.

They pivoted, shuffling the box out of the hallway and into the séance room. Like the rest of the house, the séance room had old hardwood floors and thick white molding. Unlike the rest of the house, Grandma Missouri had painted the walls a celestial blue, strewn silky pillows all over the low-slung chairs, and had a cash register by the door.

"Lies and distortions?" Grandma Missouri asked, adjusting a loosened roller and eyeing Carolina with irritation. "Child, I will have you know I don't have to lie. People wear the truth of who they are. You just have to be able to read it, and I can and Alabama knows it."

Kick knew Alabama as Aunt Aly and also That Pain In My Neck because that's what Kick's mother called her. Aunt Aly had a lot of opinions, and while Georgia didn't share any of them, the two women *did* share the family's naming legacy. All of Grandma Missouri's girls were named after states because Grandma Missouri's mother named *her* girls after states and tradition was tradition.

Or it *was* until Georgia named her daughter Karis.

And Karis renamed herself Kick.

Grandma Missouri popped open the box and started rummaging through it, humming tunelessly. Carolina and Kick exchanged a quick look. Usually when their grandmother started humming like that, she was coming up with a plan. Sometimes that worked out well for the girls.

And just as often it didn't.

Carolina brushed off her hands on her skirt. "Can we go now?"

"By all means," Grandma Missouri said, pulling wrapping out of the box. "Don't let my lies and distortions stop you."

Carolina rolled her eyes. "Are you ready?" she asked Kick. "I'm supposed to walk you to school."

"I was going to take the bus."

"There isn't one. Not even five hundred people in Bohring, remember? I'm supposed to show you the shortcut."

Kick felt the overwhelming need for a dramatic sigh. Carolina looked as if she quite agreed, but she held her ground—probably because she had to. If Georgia was big on Important Moments, Aunt Aly was big on Doing the Right Thing. It was nice until you realized you *were* one of those things. Being her cousin's good deed made Kick feel embarrassed and irritable—and a tiny bit grateful because she really didn't want to walk to school alone.

Which made her even more irritable.

"Fine. Whatever." Kick dashed into the hallway to pack her book bag. Carolina followed along and watched her tuck new pencils and new folders next to her very old notebook of experiments.

"What is that?" her cousin wanted to know.

"A notebook."

"I can see *that*, but it's gross and falling apart. Why haven't you thrown it away?"

Because my parents gave it to me, Kick wanted to explain. Because it had all the experiments she would conduct one day.

"Because I like it," she said, and that was true as well. "Don't tell me what to do."

"Well, hurry up and I won't have to." Carolina picked up her pink backpack and slung it over one shoulder. "I don't want to be late."

Kick didn't want to be late either. She already felt queasy, like the time she didn't eat breakfast and then got on a plane with her mother. It was *not* a good sign. Forget being the New Girl; if she barfed on the first day of school she'd be the Weirdo for sure.

Kick shouldered her backpack and followed Carolina out the front door. "Bye, Grandma Missouri!"

"Hmpf hmpf!" Grandma Missouri responded, which might have been "Bye, Kick!" but could also have been

"Stupid crystal ball!" It was hard to tell when Grandma Missouri had her head in a box.

The screen door slapped shut behind Carolina. "Hurry up!"

Kick ran after her.

GRANDMA MISSOURI'S
PREDICTION

"The curse is coming. You need to prepare."

Carolina didn't let up. Outside, the humidity might have turned the air soup-thick, but she ran on.

And on.

Kick raced after her. Ribbons flying, Carolina beat Kick across the Hollows' rickety bridge, but Kick caught up with her when they reached Figgis's favorite mud hole. Then Carolina beat her again as they pounded up the dusty path to the dusty road.

They cut across the road to the shortcut that ran along the swamp's edge. All around them, crickets shrilled and tall grasses waved on overwarm breezes. Not that the girls noticed. They were running as fast as they could, heading for the opening in the trees that would lead up to the side street that would lead them on to the school.

Almosttherealmosthere! Kick pumped her knees harder. Carolina grabbed her elbow, skidding in the dirt as she hauled them both to a stop under the shade of a silver maple.

"Careful! Your shoelaces are untied!"

"They are *not!*"

"Oops, my mistake." Carolina bent in half, grabbing her side. "I was just looking out for you. I would've won no matter what. You're tired. I can tell."

"I'm *not* tired," Kick lied, trying not to pant so much. Grandma Missouri said Kick needed to play outside more and play with her chemistry set less. Grandma Missouri might have been right. Then again, Grandma Missouri also said the cousins needed to get along, and Kick was reasonably certain it was scientifically *impossible* to get along with Carolina.

"Whatever." Carolina straightened, sniffed, and powered up the grassy embankment. It was the end of the shortcut and spilled them onto a tree-lined street. Kick's cousin walked off to the left, pink skirt frothing around her knees.

Muttering, Kick followed.

Bohring Elementary and Middle School was tucked between leafy oaks, and even though it was early, Kick was glad for the shade. The heat was shimmery in the distance, and when more kids ran past, their shoes stirred up brittle pikes of grass. Ahead, the playground's spiny, spiky fence edged into view, and Carolina stopped, turning around so fast Kick nearly ran into her.

"What?" she panted.

Carolina wouldn't look at her. Her hands kept flexing around her backpack straps as if she were afraid she would lift away, and her eyes kept wandering to the other kids. She was here, but she was already thinking about being somewhere else—*anywhere* else. Kick's heart sank because she knew that look. She knew it because her mother wore it so often.

"Look," Carolina said at last, picking at her fingernails and then picking at her lower lip. "I'm really sorry, but you can't walk in with me."

Kick blinked. "Why not?"

"Because I can't be seen with you. It's hard enough having Grandma Missouri as my grandma, but Jenna Jane has already told everyone you're weird."

"How . . . ?" Kick trailed off. She wasn't sure she wanted to know how Jenna Jane managed that. Or maybe she did. Maybe she needed to study gossip. It seemed to be faster than the speed of light—which was supposed to be super-fast, according to Kick's books, but maybe wasn't nearly that fast after all.

"I'm really sorry," Carolina repeated, her eyes stuck to her feet now. "It's just . . . things are hard for me too, and I don't want to make it worse. I'll see you around, okay?"

"Okay." But it wasn't okay at all. Kick stood under a fat oak tree and watched her cousin disappear into the schoolyard. The bigger kids were running around in packs, and the younger kids were getting in the way, and no one seemed to notice Carolina slip past them.

Maybe that's what her cousin wanted?

Kick didn't know what she wanted except, well, maybe she did. She wanted this school year to be different. Clearly, that hadn't worked out so well with the Jennas, but a good scientist wouldn't stop at one failure.

If you want a different result, try a different approach. It was her father's voice in her head, clear as day, and it made Kick's shoulders square. He always said that when an experiment went wrong or when a prediction fizzled out. It worked for him then, and it would work for Kick now.

Hopefully.

Maybe.

Definitely, Kick told herself as she marched straight toward the spiny, spiky schoolyard gate and all the children playing behind it—who didn't notice her any more than they'd noticed her cousin.

She dodged left, barely avoiding a boy stomping on ants, then ducked right, almost getting tangled in a game of jump rope. One of the girls glared at her but kept singing in time to the rope's swing:

"One, two, monsters coming for you!
Three, four, they're outside your door!
Five, six, first it smells like Styx!

Seven, eight, hear the growls of fate!

Nine, ten, see the monsters again!"

Kick scowled. *Smells like* sticks? *Is that supposed to be a technical term because—*

A glass-bright soap bubble drifted past her face. It was so pretty, Kick gasped. Then she gasped again because it stank. Horribly.

A shadow fell across her. It belonged to a boy.

A *big* boy.

He crammed his bubble wand into its clear plastic container and leaned in. "Well, hey there, friend."

Kick paused. She'd wanted friends. Was it really going to be this easy? "Um, hello to you too . . . friend."

His ham-pink freckles twitched when he smiled. "Might I interest you in a lucky penny? As you know, the hundred years is up and the curse is upon us. These, however, ward off all evil, younger siblings, and current curses."

Everything inside Kick flattened. "There's no such thing as curses."

"Ah. You're new here, aren't you? Let me help you out; every hundred years, all the kids of Bohring—"

"I know the story. It's still not true."

"It *is* true, and I'm selling you salvation for a dollar."

She gaped. "A dollar! It's a penny!"

The older boy—Lucky Penny Boy, as Kick was beginning to think of him—pulled back. He had dark slashes for brows, and one arched when he looked at her. "The upcharge covers the blessings placed on the pennies—they don't come naturally lucky, you know. I have to work with them, train 'em up." He snatched a glance behind him as if keeping an eye out for teachers. "The upcharge also covers my risk."

"I don't need a lucky penny."

"Suit yourself." He gave her a mean little smirk. "Monster green would probably be an improvement on you anyway."

"It probably would," Kick countered, stomping inside the school with her head held high.

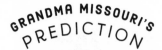

"I see a very poor decision in your future."

Mrs. Flagg's classroom was crowded. There were kids in the desks, kids in the rows between the desks, kids talking to each other over the desks, and no one was sitting down.

Well, except for Carolina. She was on one side of the classroom, and since there didn't seem to be assigned seating, Kick picked a seat on the other side. They both pretended they didn't see each other.

It was so busy in there, Kick almost believed it. She took out her new notebooks, her old notebook, and her pencils. Then she rearranged herself so she could tuck the old notebook into her lap. She never knew when ideas might come to her. It was best to be prepared.

Bzzzrrriiinnnggg!

She winced. The school bell screeched like Butler when someone slammed his tail in a door.

"Well, hey." Jenna H. paused by Kick's desk. Today, she wore a bright pink T-shirt. "I was just thinking about you."

A tiny chill ran down the back of Kick's neck, but she tried to sound unconcerned. "Oh?"

Jenna B. peeked over Jenna H.'s shoulder. She also wore a bright pink T-shirt.

Noticing a definite trend here, Kick thought.

"We have a sleepover at Jenna Jane's every Friday," Jenna H. continued. "It's *so* much fun. Maybe you should come?"

Kick's heart double-thumped. "Um . . ."

The girls stepped back, and Jenna Jane pushed between them. Her T-shirt was the brightest pink of all.

"What do you think, Jenna Jane?" Jenna H. asked, ponytail swinging. "Should we invite Kick to your party?"

Jenna Jane looked Kick over—taking just enough time so Kick could think, *pleasepleaseplease*—before a slow smile walked up one corner of her mouth. "No way."

The words blew Kick empty. She opened her mouth and nothing came out. She tried to breathe and couldn't.

It made the Jennas grin.

"Good morning, class!"

The Jennas giggled and pushed past, taking seats a few rows behind her. Kick pressed her shaking hands on top of her desk as their teacher, Mrs. Flagg, shuffled to the front of the classroom. Mrs. Flagg had faded yellow hair, a soft tummy that pushed through the blue fabric of her dress, and a smile so real it squinted up her eyes as she faced her students and asked, "Is everyone ready to make it a great day?"

"Yes, Mrs. Flagg!" the whole class sang.

Well, the whole class except for Kick. She was eyeing Lucky Penny Boy, who kept rolling one of his supposedly lucky pennies from knuckle to knuckle.

Mrs. Flagg smiled some more, her attention traveling over the students and landing on Kick. "There you are! Karis Wint—"

"It's Kick."

Her teacher blinked. She touched two fingers to her eyeglasses and squinted at the paper. "Oh, yes. Kick. I see it now."

Kick highly doubted Mrs. Flagg saw anything—not with the way she kept adjusting her glasses—but she kept it to herself. She studied how there were magenta threads stuck to Mrs. Flagg's blue dress and smudges of glitter on Mrs. Flagg's thumb, and wondered what predictions her grandmother would pull from those details.

"In order to be psychic," Grandma Missouri was always saying in her deepest voice, "you have to see the truth inside a person—but the truth is usually written *on* them if you know where to look."

Bet she enjoys arts and crafts, Kick thought.

The teacher walked to the front of the whiteboard and folded her hands. "Class, we have a new student. This is Kick Winter. I hope y'all make her feel welcome."

No one said anything, but that didn't seem to bother Mrs. Flagg. She turned to Kick, and her wide smile became even wider. "Would you like to come up and tell us a few things about yourself?"

Kick thought she would rather lick a hot Bunsen burner, but she didn't say that. After all, it wasn't really Mrs. Flagg's fault she asked this. Kick was pretty sure making new kids talk about themselves was in the teachers' manual, and as she now knew, if something was in the manual you had to do it.

"Come along, dear," Mrs. Flagg urged. Someone in the back sniggered—someone who sounded an awful lot like one of the Jennas.

Get going, Kick told herself. She pushed herself to her feet and dragged her way down the aisle. It was even worse up front. She looked at the class, and the class looked at her.

Well, Carolina looked at the floor. She was holding herself very still like she was worried a bee was going to land on her.

Or that something horrible was happening.

Relatable, Kick thought, clearing her throat. "Um, I'm Kick Winter and . . ." *And I like chemistry? And I conduct experiments? And I will be writing down weird habits you might have and I might want to study?* Kick couldn't say any of these things, which of course meant those things were the *only* things she could think about.

"It's okay, dear," said Mrs. Flagg, leaning a little toward her. It made the keys she wore on a lanyard around her neck swing forward, jingling. "Take your time. We want to hear all about you."

"Oh, yah," Jenna Jane said. "Tell us how *special* you are, Kick."

The class tittered, and their teacher looked around in confusion. She had no way of knowing Jenna Jane was being spiteful. Just like she had no way of knowing the way Jenna Jane said "special" wasn't special at all.

But Kick knew, and knowing made her knees shake.

Mrs. Flagg smiled at Kick. "Go ahead, dear."

She took a deep breath and caught herself staring at her teacher's glittery hands again.

"Dear?" the teacher asked, her smile starting to strain. She was worried.

That makes two of us, Kick thought, beginning to sweat. She had to make a decision: hide or fight. *If you want a different result, you have to try a different approach.*

Which meant if Jenna Jane was going to make Kick out to be special, then Kick was going to have to *be* special.

She lifted her chin. "I'm Kick Winter, and I'm psychic."

GRANDMA MISSOURI'S PREDICTION

"Go big or go home."

Mrs. Flagg's eyes bulged. "Now, now, dear, let's not tell stories—"

"Wait!" Kick pressed the back of one hand to her forehead just as she'd seen Grandma Missouri do dozens of times before. "I'm having a vision! A vision of . . ." She dropped her hand and squinted at her teacher. "A vision of you and something sparkly? Yes, *sparkly*! Like gold in the sunshine. Like jewels under clear water."

Someone made a gagging sound, and again, Kick was pretty sure that someone was Jenna Jane. She concentrated harder on Mrs. Flagg. "Are you an artist?"

"Well," their teacher said, face and neck going pink. "I dabble a little. Crafts mostly."

Kick stared, a funny feeling uncurling in her chest. Was it excitement? Nervousness? She wasn't sure. It should be triumph. She'd guessed right. She was *good* at this, and that felt almost as fantastic as the few amazed gasps that went up among the students.

She sneaked a glance at them and realized a few of the girls' expressions had changed. Before, their eyes had bounced over Kick like she was furniture. Now they looked at her like she was *someone*.

Someone special.

Kick touched Mrs. Flagg's sleeve the way Grandma Missouri always did when a client revealed a bit more information. "You should keep it up, Mrs. Flagg. It's very important to pursue your passions."

"Is it?" Behind her glasses, Mrs. Flagg's eyes were wide and watery, and Kick paused. This suddenly felt a bit wrong. Her answer seemed to really mean something to Mrs. Flagg.

"It *is*," she said at last. "It's important to *you*."

And that was true. Kick thought about telling Mrs. Flagg how much chemistry and experiments were important to her, and how much Kick understood how Mrs. Flagg felt, but she didn't. Science hadn't won her very many friends, but being psychic seemed like it might. Two girls in the front row were already smiling at Kick, and Kick couldn't help but smile back.

"Is it important to the spirits too?" Mrs. Flagg whispered.

Kick chewed her lower lip. This was taking it a bit far, wasn't it? Then again, as Grandma Missouri would say,

Kick was already in it, so—"Absolutely, it's important to them," she said.

"Why?" The question came from the back of the classroom and belonged to a boy with a single eyebrow growing straight across his forehead. "Why would they care?"

"Hush, Cash," Mrs. Flagg said, eyes never swerving from Kick.

"But—"

"I said hush!"

Cash fell silent. The class fell silent. Everyone seemed to be waiting on Kick's final prediction, and . . . well . . . she didn't have one. This was usually the part where Grandma Missouri asked if the customer wanted to pay with cash or check.

"Art makes you happy, right?" Kick asked.

Mrs. Flagg gave a jerky nod. "Yes."

"Then you should keep doing it."

"I will! Anything else?"

Kick wrinkled her nose, trying to think of anything that topped being a psychic and then realized Mrs. Flagg wasn't asking for Kick to talk about herself anymore—she wanted Kick to talk about the spirits. Kick shrugged. "Uh, nothing."

"Well, that was very impressive." Mrs. Flagg clapped, and after a brief hesitation, the students clapped too. Lucky Penny Boy probably clapped the hardest. "Very, very impressive, Kick Winter. I'm sure your grandmother must be so proud. You may sit down."

Head held high, Kick walked toward her desk, sliding into her seat with clammy hands and an overfull chest. Mrs. Flagg started talking about projects and homework and what to expect over the next few weeks, but no one was listening.

The girl to Kick's left was smiling at her, and the boy to her right gave her a tiny wave. The kids ahead of her kept peeking around, and the kids behind her, well, Kick wasn't sure what they were doing, but she *felt* like they were watching her too. Everyone seemed interested.

Well, everyone except for Carolina. She looked as disgusted as Jenna Jane.

Kick ignored them, something that proved remarkably easy to do since, for the first time in as long as she could remember, people seemed to want to be her friend.

Too bad it didn't last.

***

It was quite possibly the most exciting first day of class ever. With a beginning like that, Kick started to think her sixth-grade year would continue in a blaze of glory.

Or crash-land into boring, she thought a few hours later, looking over the notes for her upcoming classes. No baking-soda volcano, but there *would* be cloning cabbages— which had the potential to be very cool, but it was *cabbages.* There was also a Bohring town history assignment, and a bunch of assigned books for reading. None of them sounded remotely interesting.

"You can't find *anything* you like?" Mrs. Flagg asked.

Kick noticed how her teacher's mouth went thin when she didn't believe something.

Which was too bad because this was the truth. Kick really wasn't big on reading. She liked doing. "No," she repeated. "Nothing."

"Well, we'll just have to work on that!" Mrs. Flagg clapped her hands to get the other students' attention. "Time for science! Is everyone ready to check on their cabbage clones? You can sit anywhere you like as long as you work quietly. Kick? You'll have to find a lab partner to work with."

Joy, Kick thought, slouching lower in her seat as everyone else got up. The Jennas took their cabbage experiment to a spot by the window, Carolina took hers back to her desk, and a girl to Kick's left nudged her.

"Would you like to work with us?" she asked. "I'm Natalie May. This is Mia," she added as a shorter girl joined them, carrying a metal tray with plastic baggies of cabbage chunks.

"What you did with Mrs. Flagg was *so* cool," Mia breathed as she dragged a chair closer.

"You think so?" Kick tried not to smile too hard.

"Yah," Natalie May added, tossing her long box braids

over one shoulder and adjusting her sparkly headband. "I could never do something so amazing."

"Thanks!" Kick leaned over, studying their experiment. "Uh . . . what exactly is supposed to be going on here?" Because whatever it was, it didn't look like it was going very well. Two of the baggies had rotting cabbage bits in them. The rest looked like they were sweating to death.

Mia frowned. "I was supposed to blow a little bit of air into them, but I forgot. I didn't think it would matter, but I guess it did."

"Oh, yeah." Kick nodded. "They would've needed the carbon dioxide from your breath."

"Really?"

"I'm guessing." She wasn't, but who was counting? Well, normally, Kick would've been, but that was then and this was now and *now* had two girls who seemed to want to be friends.

"Ladies?" Mrs. Flagg looked up from the papers she was grading, eyeglasses hanging off the tip of her nose. "Are you recording your findings or socializing?"

Kick focused on the two cabbage stems that *did* seem to be growing, but she felt so round and full and happy she couldn't concentrate. She clutched her data chart, gaze skittering around the room . . . and landing on Cash of the enormous eyebrow.

He was talking to himself, tugging at his ear like a mosquito circled him. No one else seemed to notice.

And Kick couldn't look away.

Their eyes met. "Do you hear that?" Cash mouthed, pawing at his forehead—or maybe his eyebrow.

"Quiet!" Mrs. Flagg demanded.

Kick flinched, looking back down at her chart. "Hear that"? She hadn't heard anything, but she definitely saw the panic in Cash's expression—and every time she remembered it, a shiver zinged down her spine.

"Be careful what you wish for."

Popularity certainly had its perks. Sure, Kick was still the New Girl, but she wasn't the Girl Who Sat Alone at Lunch anymore. In natural science, everyone wanted to be her partner. In gym, everyone wanted to pass her the ball.

I should've pretended to be psychic years ago, Kick thought, and when the bell rang for the end of school, she walked out of class with Natalie May and Mia at her side.

The girls stepped into the sunshine just as Lucky Penny Boy blew past. LPB—whose real name was Jefferson Burr and who also happened to be the mayor's son—slammed his shoulder into Kick's, nearly sending her flying.

"Lucky pennies!" he cried, a plastic bubble container in one hand and a roll of pennies in the other. "Get your lucky pennies!"

Natalie May gasped. "Are you okay?"

"Fine." Kick rubbed her shoulder and glared at Jefferson.

He glared right back and yelled, "Avoid the curse with your new lucky penny!"

"Isn't he kind of big for sixth grade?" she asked.

"Jefferson's repeating," Mia explained. "Says it's his favorite so far."

"Oh."

"I need to get one of those pennies," Natalie May said, adjusting her sparkly headband. "Maybe two. The hundred years *is* up after all."

Kick paused. She wasn't sure where to begin, but she was fairly certain it wasn't with *Lucky pennies are even more ridiculous than curses*.

Even if it *was* true.

"One, two, monsters coming for you!" The girls with the jump rope were at it again, every leap flinging dust into the air. "Three, four, they're outside your door!"

"You're not helping!" Natalie May yelled as they passed.

"Five, six, first it smells like Styx!"

"I don't get it," Kick said. "Sticks? What do sticks smell like?"

"*Styx*," Mia corrected. "Like the River Styx. We studied it in history. The Greeks believed it separated our world from the underworld. Dead people had to cross it."

"Oh." Kick thought it over. "Well, bonus points for the reference, I guess, but it's still a pretty lame threat. Smells and growls? What's next? Dinner's going to taste funny?"

She looked at Natalie May and Mia, hoping for agreement and instead caught them exchanging a surprised glance. "What?"

"Nothing." Mia's dark brown fingers tugged the ends of her hair. "I just would've thought you, of all people, would *know* what's next."

"Uh, that's because I'm not psychic all the time. I just get certain stuff. I don't know anything about the curse."

Which was true.

"I'm more of a spirit communicator."

Which was not true. But it seemed to make the other girls relax—or it did until the jump rope chant started up again.

"Nine, ten, see the monsters again!"

"Let's get out of here," Kick said, and Mia and Natalie May followed her through the schoolyard's spiny, spiky gate. It was swelteringly hot, but Main Street (which was really like Only Street) was busy as ever. Little old ladies marched in and out of the Curl Up and Dye. The mayor swept the hardware store's front step, stopping to shake hands with anyone who walked by, and trucks with massive tires crowded every parking space in front of the Grimp and Myer. It was like any other day.

So why couldn't Kick shake off the prickle creeping down the back of her neck?

Because creepy rhymes are the backbone of any good horror

movie, she told herself. She trailed up the sidewalk with Natalie May and Mia, sticking to the shade and knowing—*knowing*—she shouldn't ask.

But she just couldn't help herself.

"What did you mean 'what's next'?"

Another glance darted between Natalie May and Mia. This one uncomfortable. *No,* Kick realized. *Reluctant.* They were scared to even talk about the legend.

"There was this witch," Mia said at last.

"What?"

"A couple hundred years ago, some kids accused a local woman of witchcraft, and it got her thrown in jail. The townspeople were afraid to give her a trial, but they were also afraid to let her go—"

"So she died in jail," Natalie May whispered, eyes going big as she leaned closer. "Maybe because someone helped her. You know, *helped* her."

"Well, I don't know personally," Kick said. "But I understand where you're going with it. You're trying to say someone killed her."

Mia's knuckles whitened as she gripped her backpack straps. "And right before she died, she cursed the town: Every hundred years, all of Bohring's kids would turn into monsters."

"That's—" *That's a long time to wait for payback,* Kick started to say. Luckily, she caught herself. "That's awful."

The girls nodded. "I know, right?" Natalie May said. "It's like blaming the rest of us for the Jennas."

"The point *is*," Mia continued, "the hundred years is up. The curse could come to life at any time now, and we'll know because of the smell."

Kick blinked, blinked again. "I'm sorry . . . the *smell*?"

The girls nodded grimly. "It's just like the rhyme: First you smell the Styx, then you hear the growls."

And then you check yourself for heatstroke, Kick thought, and mentally smacked herself. She hadn't known Natalie May and Mia for long, but she'd known them long enough to know they were smart girls. They wouldn't be taken in by just anything. Maybe belief and truth were closer than she'd realized.

Something else to study, she thought.

Natalie May hesitated, nibbling her lower lip. "Are you getting anything from the spirits about the curse?"

She was trying for light, but it was another loaded question—one that was so much worse than when Grandma Missouri asked if Dad had bought Kick that experiment book. *This* question burrowed deep into Kick. For a second, she was breathless.

"Kick?" Natalie May took Kick's hand, and her palm was icy.

"The spirits would never let anything happen to you," she told her. "You're safe."

Which wasn't even a lie. Well, it wasn't much of one. They *were* safe. There was no such thing as curses.

Natalie May's grin stretched wide as her face. Wider. "I'm so glad we're friends!"

"Me too!" Mia added.

You should feel guilty about that, Kick thought, but she didn't. She didn't have room for it. Natalie May and Mia were shining in every corner of her mind. Besides, the promise changed everything. The girls relaxed. They believed her.

Afternoon sun cast golden coins of light across the sidewalk, and as they walked on, Natalie May didn't talk about needing lucky pennies. She told Kick how much she loved horses, and Mia told Kick how she wanted to try out for the school play, and they *both* encouraged Kick to try out with her.

It was easy, comfortable. Having friends wasn't anything like she'd dreamed.

It was better.

"Who are you going to believe? Me, or your lying eyes?"

"See you tomorrow," Mia said when they reached the top of the school's road. The other girls turned for town—briefly Kick could see her cousin ahead of them, but then Carolina turned right and disappeared into the heat-wavy horizon—and Kick ducked off the road. She scrambled down the embankment, taking the shortcut to the Hollows.

Tangled branches might have hidden the sun, but they held the heat as Kick skirted the swamp's muddy edge. Everything went thick and hushed.

Fanning her face with one hand, she tried to focus on her day. Pretending to be psychic had been an extremely successful experiment. She had friends now. Things were looking up.

But there were also the Jennas.

And the curse.

And the more Kick thought about the curse, the *closer*

the trees seemed to creep on either side of the muddy path.

Monsters could hide in them, a tiny voice in Kick's head breathed.

"Not likely," she told the tiny voice. The thing was, if she were being technical—which was Kick's favorite way to be—Bohring looked like the kind of place that *would* have monsters and curses.

It was the effect of the swamp. It surrounded the Hollows, where the tiny cottage sat high on stilts. It oozed toward the town, where it lingered at the edges, and during the rainy season, it overflowed the roads. The swamp was always there.

Like it was waiting.

Which, of course, it wasn't. It was just a swamp.

It's the presentation that makes it feel like it's more, Kick thought, but she sped up a bit as she thought it. Clearly, nature was like being a fake psychic: You had to have the right accessories—in this case, kudzu vines, mosquitoes, and curses.

Not a bad observation, she decided, fingers itching for the notebook secure in her book bag. *I should write that one down. Later.*

Like at home.

Behind the closed front door.

Behind the closed and *locked* front door because Kick kept feeling a tickling at the back of her neck.

Like she was being watched.

"There's no such thing as monsters," she muttered, and *that* was when she heard the footsteps.

She whirled, spotting two boys scurrying down the shortcut after her. *Twins,* Kick realized, taking in their almost-matching faces a heartbeat after she took in their identical WrestleMania T-shirts. They had sun-bleached-blond hair, mosquito-bitten arms, and their smiles promised mayhem.

"You're the psychic," the first one said, grinning. He dashed the back of his hand against his nose. "We were trying to catch up with you."

"Oh, yeah?"

"Yeah," said the second. "We got questions."

Kick struggled not to frown. In this particular case, questions weren't good. At all. "Who are you?"

The first one grinned. "I'm Buddy Macon. This is Buford. Don't freak out. I know we're kind of a big deal around here."

Kick paused, racking her brain for a reference to Buddy or Buford Macon and finding, well, nothing. "I'll try to contain myself. What do you want to know?"

"Winning lottery-ticket numbers for starters," Buddy said, "then the answers to tomorrow's math test and Jenna Jane's hand in marriage."

Buford snorted. "Dude, she's psychic. She doesn't grant wishes."

Off in the distance, a cricket trilled and suddenly fell silent. Actually, now that Kick thought about it, the whole swamp had gone silent. No birds. No bugs. Nothing. That was weird.

But anyone who wanted to marry Jenna Jane was weirder.

"I can't really help you with any of that," she told them. "My purpose is more, uh, noble."

Buford's face screwed up tight. "Then what's the use in being psychic?"

"And what's more noble than marrying Jenna Jane?" Buddy asked.

Kick looked at Buford.

Buford shrugged. "He's weird, but he's family."

"You have no idea how much I get that." She turned to Buddy. "You're on your own with Jenna Jane."

Buddy scowled, eyes narrowing. He opened his mouth and—

He gasped. "What was that?"

"What's *what*?" But then suddenly Kick knew. What was that *smell*? It was awful. It was *worse* than awful.

"He who smelt it dealt it." Buddy elbowed his twin.

"Didn't," Buford hissed.

"Did."

"Didn't!"

"Shut up!" Kick circled slowly, taking in the swamp around them. The wind picked up, making the trees rustle, their branches rubbing together like a thousand sighs. It should have swept the stench away, but somehow it made it worse.

Buddy gagged. "It's—it's like a porta potty in August!"

"Like rotten eggs!"

"It's the *smell*!"

"That's not a thing," Kick snapped, forcing herself in another tight circle. She turned and turned, eyes searching and searching. This part of the swamp was always pretty shallow, but during late summer, it was almost entirely mud and scraggly undergrowth. Nothing should have been able to hide.

Unless it's behind that fallen cypress tree, she realized, pulse pounding. The tree was massive. Almost anything could hide behind the moss-covered trunk.

Buford pawed at his face. "It's the smell! It's the curse!"

"There is no curse!" Kick snapped.

But there *was* a stench, and no amount of denial could sweep away something that *did* smell like a porta potty in August and *did* smell like rotten eggs. The wind whipped around them once more. A branch snapped.

"It's getting worse!" Buford cried.

It was. Kick inhaled hard, the smell pressing closer as something behind the fallen cypress moved. Ripples in the water spiraled outward like something heavy had stepped into the depths.

"Something's in there!" Buddy whispered.

"Of course something's in there," Kick whispered back. "Lots of somethings live in the swamp."

Splash!

It came from their left, nowhere near the cypress, but all three of them jumped. "Aieeeeee!" screamed Buford— or maybe it was Buddy. Kick wasn't sure. She couldn't drag her eyes from the tree. What was going *on*?

Something awful, her brain supplied.

"Besides awful," she said as another gust of wind shook the swamp.

"Run for it!" Buddy/Buford cried. The twins bolted in the opposite direction, off the path and into the shallows. For a heartbeat, Kick nearly followed them.

Then she stabbed her sneakers into the muddy path.

I'm not running from a smell, she told herself.

Grrrrrr!

The growl was low and chilling, and it wasn't *getting* closer.

It's already here.

Kick spun around for the Hollows. She slipped, slipped again, and righted herself, taking off down the path as something heavy splashed into the water. *Fasterfasterfaster!*

But she wasn't fast enough.

Behind her, branches popped like gunfire. The splashes were speeding up.

Catching up.

Kick ran harder, backpack bouncing from side to side as she raced down the path. Sunlight forked through the thinning trees. She wheeled around the last turn and saw the grassy embankment just ahead. Knees pumping hard, she scrambled up the incline, hit the dusty dirt road at a dead run, and tore across the crooked bridge.

Grrrrrr!

Close. So close, she almost tripped again. *Don't stop! Don't look! Almost there!* She scaled the splintery steps in one leap and hurled herself through the front door.

"Good heavens, child!" Grandma Missouri bellowed from the séance room as Kick hurled herself through the front door. "What are you *doing*?"

Running for my life, Kick thought, panting.

But when she looked behind her, nothing was there.

A humid breeze stirred through the swamp, dragging the smell of swamp water and pine trees with it. The dusty dirt road was empty. The crooked bridge was empty. Somewhere close by Figgis splashed.

That didn't just happen, Kick thought, but no matter how many times she told herself this, she didn't believe a word of it.

GRANDMA MISSOURI'S
PREDICTION

10

"No, dear, if one door closes and another
one opens, that means you're living
in a haunted house. Time to move."

Tuesday morning came to the Hollows as it usually always
did: blinding sunshine, overfull breezes, and a hungry alligator. Figgis only needed to eat once a week, but he wasn't
one to suffer in silence. He made so much noise thrashing
around in his bog, Kick could forget what happened yesterday.

Well, *almost*.

She held her nose with one hand while she fished
expired chicken cutlets out of their plastic cooler. It didn't
help much. The rotten chicken smelled awful, but Figgis
clearly didn't agree. Every time she pitched one off the
porch, he dove for it, roaring ferociously. Or maybe hap-
pily. Or maybe ferocious and happy were the same thing
for alligators.

Finally finished, Kick tossed the metal tongs into an

empty flower box. There were five or six boxes to pick from because in addition to being a grandma who didn't bake, Grandma Missouri didn't garden. She did, however, have a great love for taxidermied animals and found it relaxing to make clothes for them.

Kick peered over the wooden railing, watching Figgis and smelling the swamp. *No unexplainable horrible smells today,* she thought.

And even more importantly, no unexplainable horrible growls.

"What on earth are you staring at? Come eat breakfast!" Grandma Missouri yelled through the open kitchen window. Grandma Missouri probably thought Kick was acting strangely, and as far as Kick was concerned, she could continue to think it. She wasn't about to admit she'd smelled or heard anything in the swamp. It came too close to admitting her grandmother was right.

Still, she thought—and kind of hated the thought all the same—*it would be nice to talk to someone about it.*

"There's no such thing as curses or monsters," she whispered, putting the lid back on the cooler and waving good-bye to Figgis. The alligator blew bubbles in response.

Inside, Grandma Missouri was tearing around the kitchen, preparing breakfast. She wore wide-legged trousers and a white silk blouse, and her cane had a racing stripe down it (*So I look like I'm going fast,* she would always say). Anyone else would've been frazzled in the over-warm kitchen. Grandma Missouri was ready for her close-up.

Maybe she is *magic,* Kick thought, narrowing her eyes. It might explain the squeaking thing that lived in her purse.

"Wash your hands," Grandma Missouri said.

Like I need reminding. Kick turned the water as hot as it could go and scoured her fingers. The tongs kept her from having to touch the raw chicken, but the lingering smell always made her queasy.

"Eat," Grandma Missouri said, passing her a plate of toast and scrambled eggs. Kick took it to the table and moved her grandmother's sewing around until she had room to eat. Larry and Gary—her grandmother's stuffed squirrels— were getting new outfits. It looked like Larry was getting an opera cape.

Or is that Gary? Kick wondered, taking a bite of toast.

Bing! Biiinnnggg!

"Miss Missouri?" a voice called. "You home?"

"In the kitchen!" Grandma Missouri smoothed down her trousers and blouse and dropped her voice to a murmur: "Where else would I be at this godforsaken hour?"

Kick opened her mouth, but her grandmother held up one finger. "Not a word, young lady. Not. A. Word."

Kick deflated, retreating to the kitchen table as Mrs. Patricia Conroy came in. Mrs. Conroy believed in high heels, higher hair, and the psychic readings of Miss Sudavee Bark, the *other* fake psychic in Bohring.

Miss Sudavee had a cottage between the Bohring County Insurance Company and the hardware store—or she *did* until she divorced her husband and he burned it to the ground. Now she had a single-wide trailer between the Bohring County Insurance Company and hardware store. It was bright yellow with exposed cinder-block pillars and a colony of feral cats living underneath it. Miss Sudavee said they were drawn to her spiritual energy. Kick was pretty sure they were drawn to the tuna she put out.

Regardless, it was surprising to see Mrs. Conroy at the Hollows. Even if Grandma Missouri acted like it wasn't. She gave Mrs. Conroy a big smile and patted the closest kitchen chair like they did this all the time. "Why, hello there, dear. I wondered when you would arrive."

Mrs. Conroy clutched the top of her purse with both hands. She was shaking. "Oh, Miss Missouri, it's happening."

Kick paused, scrambled eggs halfway to her mouth.

"What's happening?" her grandmother asked.

"The *curse*! Did you hear about the smell? And the *growls*?" Kick dropped her fork. Grandma Missouri cut her a glare. "First, the stench crept all over town last night, then came the growls. They were *right outside my bedroom window*. All night."

"Did anyone see anything?" Kick asked.

Her grandmother cut her another glare, but Mrs. Conroy didn't seem to notice. Her face had gone the color of sodden ashes. "Nothing yet. But that's coming, isn't it? First you smell the monsters, then you hear them, and then you *see* them because you *become* one!" She took a deep breath and looked at Grandma Missouri. "I need a good-luck charm for my little girl. And Miss Sudavee is visiting her great-aunt and—and—are you any good at that sort of thing?"

Grandmother and granddaughter exchanged the briefest of glances. Grandma Missouri's said: "Are we ever?" Kick's was more like: "Here we go again."

"I mean—" Mrs. Conroy flushed bright red, and she clutched her purse like it might fly away. "I mean, Miss Sudavee says you aren't quite as blessed."

Grandma Missouri's mouth went flat. "Did she, now?"

"She also said a good-luck charm wouldn't work! She said the curse is too strong!" It was nonsense and Kick knew it was nonsense, but the panic in Mrs. Conroy's voice still made her skin push up in goose bumps.

Not to mention you smelled the stench too, she reminded herself. *And you heard the growling.* It made it more than a little difficult to call the whole thing ridiculous.

Not that Kick wasn't willing to try.

Could swamp gas move in large clouds? she wondered. Maybe—but it didn't explain the growling.

"You poor thing," Grandma Missouri said, ushering a trembling Mrs. Conroy to the kitchen table. She poured her a mug of coffee. "You must understand, I would never want to disparage a fellow practitioner of the mystical arts, *but* how much can you trust the predictions *or* good-luck charms of a psychic who can't afford the underpinnings for her trailer? Hmmm?"

Mrs. Conroy blinked, thinking this over. "That's a very good point." She flexed her fingers against her purse and seemed to relax a tiny bit. "So do you have any? Good-luck charms, I mean?"

"Of course," Grandma Missouri said, a smile as wide as her face. "We'll just need to ask the spirits for a little additional blessing." She shot her granddaughter another tiny glance, and Kick gave her an equally tiny nod.

"Now, how would you like to pay, dear?" Grandma Missouri hooked her arm around Mrs. Conroy's shoulders and steered her toward the séance room. "We take cash, check, money orders . . ."

Kick took a huge mouthful of eggs and clattered her dirty plate into the sink. *One Mississippi. Two Mississippi,* she counted, and when she reached twenty Mississippi, she leaned across the Formica counter and turned on the power to the disposal. Through the thin walls between the kitchen and séance room, Kick heard something buzz and sizzle.

"Behold!" her grandmother boomed. "The spirits are with us!"

Or Kick had discovered how to use the Hollows' faulty wiring to their advantage last summer, but really who was counting? For once, Kick certainly wasn't. Things around Bohring were getting so strange.

They were getting late too. If Kick didn't hurry, she'd miss homeroom. Standing at the front door, she stuffed her feet into her sneakers and listened to her grandmother's words drift through the séance room's door.

"Bless you and keep you," Grandma Missouri was saying in a voice that was glass-smooth and filled with hidden things.

Just like the surface of the swamp, Kick thought, the idea pulling at something deep inside her.

"Spirits, if you bless this token, give us a sign!" Grandma Missouri cried. Kick kicked the baseboard. Right on cue, the table-shaker began to shake, and she ran on to school.

"Signs are everywhere."

Crickets chirped in the long grass as Kick ran toward school. *I'm going to be late,* she thought, pushing herself faster. *I'm going to have to walk into class, and everyone's going to stare at me.*

It was not a time to linger, but even so, she still snatched glances at the swamp around her. It was just a swamp. No horrible smells. No growling. Nothing. That had to be a good sign, right?

Wrong.

And Kick knew it when she careened around the last corner, heading for the schoolyard. *Everyone* was outside—teachers, students, parents, the mayor—and *everyone* was talking all at once.

Or rather, shouting at once.

Miss Cleo—who owned the Curl Up and Dye and was known for her temper—kept shaking her fist at Mayor Burr, upper arms jiggling like broken-open cans of biscuit dough. Mr. Myer, on the other hand, kept his fists low, gripping his rust-stained apron. Only . . . was it rust? Because Kick suddenly wasn't so sure.

That's a whole new layer of creepy, she thought, scooting through the crowd. Everyone might look different—Mr. Grimp had fading red hair and a stained apron, and the office workers had almost-identical suits and deep brown skin—but *everyone* wore fear the same way.

Well, everyone did except for Mrs. Flagg and Dr. Callahan. They stood at the edge of the crowd, Mrs. Flagg holding a sobbing little girl, and Dr. Callahan watching, her hands fluttering like she didn't know where to put them.

"People!" Mayor Burr climbed two of the school steps, realized he was only a head taller than everyone else, and climbed two more. He smoothed his comb-over and shouted: "Everyone calm down!"

Everyone did not calm down. Everyone got louder. The little girl shrieked. The crowd rumbled. Kick edged between two men with stork-like legs and past a woman with toddlers hanging off either hip, eventually finding Natalie May and Mia by the spiny, spiky fence. They held identical white papers and were watching two grown-ups yell at each other. "What's going on?" Kick asked.

"I thought you were psychic." Jenna Jane shoved past,

Jenna H. and Jenna B. following closely behind. Today, they wore purple. Like emperors.

Or bruises, Kick thought, glaring at the back of Jenna Jane's shiny brown head.

Mia took her hand. "The Macon twins are missing."

For a second, Kick could not feel her feet against the ground. "Buddy and Buford?"

"Yeah." Natalie May passed Kick her sheet of white paper. It was a Missing sign, photocopied in black and white. The boys grinned up at them. Below their picture it read:

BUDDY AND BUFORD MACON MISSING!
PRESUMED CURSED!
IF SEEN, CALL THE DINER AND ASK FOR MISS RUTH!

Hands suddenly shaking, she passed the notice back to Natalie May. "I saw them yesterday afternoon. We were walking home—through the shortcut—and we smelled that smell and they ran off into the swamp."

Natalie May's jaw dropped. "They're goners for sure, then."

"But—"

"People!" Up on the steps, Mayor Burr waved his arms to get everyone's attention. "I don't want our town to be known for this!"

"Little hard to be known for anything, Burr," someone

shouted. "We aren't actually on a map. Closest thing we got is Boone, and that's twenty miles over."

The mayor scowled like he'd tasted something disgusting.

Or maybe he was about to pass out. It was entirely possible. The sun was already high, and the mayor's face was bright red and dripping. "I hear you, Earl," he said, adjusting the glossy Vote for Burr button pinned to his lapel. "I hear you, but we need to band together. There has to be a reasonable explanation for this! It could be swamp gas!"

"Exactly." Kick decided she might like the mayor after all.

"Since when does swamp gas growl?" a woman from the back yelled.

Kick frowned. Mayor Burr frowned. The crowd rumbled again. "We've all smelled stuff in the swamp," the woman continued, "but we haven't smelled *that*, and then there was the growling. It's the curse."

Another rumble.

"My friends," Mayor Burr said, smoothing his tie and then adjusting his Vote for Burr button once more. "Reporters are on their way to Bohring *even as we speak*."

A murmur rippled through the crowd. "Reporters," Mr. Grimp said, and spat into the dirt.

Trying not to gag, Kick edged closer to her friends.

"Is this really what we want to be known for?" the mayor continued. "Monsters? My friends, this is just swamp gas and a stray alligator, and we are going to look like *idiots* when it comes to light."

"And what about my sons?" The woman from the back stepped to the front, and the air around Kick tightened.

"That's Miss Ruth," Mia whispered. "She's the twins' mom."

The explanation wasn't needed. Miss Ruth looked just like her sons—blond hair and pointed chin—but she walked like she was pushing against a hurricane.

"If there's no curse," she said slowly, "then where are Buddy and Buford?"

"Well, um, I don't rightly know. I *do* know Sheriff Day and Deputy Patel will work night and day to find your boys."

"What if the monsters got them?"

What if they did? Kick wondered. It was hot, but her skin went cold. What if whatever growled at her had gone back to get the twins? *Stop it*, she told herself. *That's impossible.*

But right now, it didn't feel impossible. It felt like the truth.

"What if the curse is here?" Miss Ruth yelled. "What if it got my boys?"

Mayor Burr sputtered. The crowd sputtered . . .

And erupted.

Kick stood between her two new friends and watched the adults yell, hand gestures slicing the air, words buzzing like wasps.

"I'm gonna need another lucky penny." Natalie May ducked into the crowd in search of Jefferson.

But you don't, Kick thought. None of this monster stuff and curse stuff made any sense—and the world *always* made sense because the world could always be explained by science, and science had no room for terrible, inexplicable smells and terrible, inexplicable growling.

It should've been a comfort. And yet she still couldn't shake the worry that something far worse than monsters was beginning.

"What? I didn't say they were good signs."

The curse. Kick thought if she rolled her eyes any harder they'd stick. There was no such thing as magic or curses or dead relatives who liked to shake Grandma Missouri's dining room table to make a point. This was stupid.

It was also all anyone could talk about.

"Do you smell that?" a fifth-grader asked her friend as they walked down the hallway that afternoon. Class was done for the day, and everyone crowded toward the double doors. "Someone here's already changing into a monster."

The other fifth-grader took a deep breath and shuddered. "I can smell it too."

Kick concentrated on her sneakers. The only thing she could smell was floor polish, which was lemony.

And definitely not eye-wateringly terrible, she thought, and then was annoyed at the thought because eye-wateringly terrible smells were as ridiculous as growling monsters and hundred-year-old curses.

There *had* to be a logical explanation for all of this—the problem was, she couldn't come up with one.

"Did you hear there's a psychic in Mrs. Flagg's class?" someone to Kick's left asked.

"*Everyone* heard about the psychic."

Unease slithered through her. *Oh boy*, she thought, trotting down the school's front steps. Outside, several parents waited for their kids, tucking them close to their side as they walked home. Kick would already be halfway home herself, but Mrs. Flagg said Grandma Missouri had called the school. She was supposed to ride home with Carolina.

Afternoon light slanted through the overgrown trees, and a limp breeze tried (unsuccessfully) to stir the humidity. *Welcome to Bohring,* Kick thought, lingering by the schoolyard's edge and praying her uncle would be here soon. *It's like breathing through a wet towel.*

"That's the new girl," a girl with pigtails whispered as she and her friend walked past Kick.

New Girl. This time, it had a certain glamour to it— definitely better than being invisible, or worse, the Weirdo.

"Kick! Kick!" Natalie May ran toward Kick, backpack bouncing from side to side. It was heavy, and Natalie May had to bend in half to catch her breath. "I have a favor to ask."

Kick perked up. A favor? Like maybe doing math home-work together? Or hanging out together? Or—

"What do the spirits say about the curse now?" Natalie May asked loudly. Several kids turned to stare. "Do they say anything about what will happen to me?"

"Um . . ." Kick swallowed, throat clicking. It was one thing to pretend to be psychic *once*. She hadn't really considered doing it again. "I'm not really feeling any spirits today?"

Natalie May slumped. "Oh, please, Kick? Please? I'll be your best friend forever!"

Kick hesitated.

"Please!"

More kids were staring now. Cash stood behind some second-graders, rubbing his ear with one hand. Jefferson and some bigger boys stopped shoving each other and came close to watch. Not that Kick noticed. She couldn't look away from Natalie May, whose eyes were huge and haunted.

She was scared. If Kick did this, it would be more than pretending to be psychic. It would be reassuring her friend, which seemed like a good thing. Even so, she caught herself wavering.

"Please?" Natalie May asked.

Okay, one more time, Kick thought, lifting her palms. It didn't feel quite right, so she lifted them higher.

"Oh, spirits," she cried, and more kids stopped to

watch. Carolina was there now—the Jennas too. The crowd hummed, growing even bigger than Mrs. Flagg's class, and Kick began to sweat.

Think like Grandma Missouri, she told herself.

And suddenly reading Natalie May became easier.

Her folders and notebooks were covered in horse stickers. She had a unicorn on her backpack. . . . *And that relates how to spirits and curses?* Kick wondered, a flare of panic making her breath hitch. She brushed it aside. "Oh, *great* spirits—"

"She's just making it up!" Jenna Jane marched forward and a murmur rippled through the schoolyard. "You're such a liar!"

Kick's face went hot. "I am *not* lying! How could I have known all that stuff about Mrs. Flagg? I'm new here. I had to rely on the spirits of the beyond to tell me."

Relying on the spirits of the beyond? Somewhere in the very back of Kick's brain, she realized she was stretching it a bit with that one, but she also knew she couldn't stop now.

She lifted her chin even higher, daring Jenna Jane to contradict her, and honestly, brazening it out wasn't a bad plan.

Until Jenna Jane smirked. "Fine. If you're a real psychic, then you should know how to get rid of the curse."

"There's no such thing as—"

"As what?" Jenna Jane's smile ate up her face. "No such thing as *what*?"

Kick paused. The denial had leaped up quickly, but now that she'd taken a breath, she wasn't sure if pretending to be psychic meant she *also* had to pretend to believe in curses.

Jenna Jane certainly seemed to think so. Her eyes gleamed as she watched Kick. "Well? Why not use your powers for good? Get rid of the curse. Everybody's scared of it."

Everybody was also staring. Kick could feel their eyes crawl over her. It made her face go even hotter.

"It's true," Natalie May whispered, patting Kick's arm like they'd been best friends for years. It was everything Kick wanted, and yet her stomach stayed around her feet. "You would be doing the whole town a favor to get rid of it. I don't want to be a monster."

Jenna Jane took another step toward Kick. "Do it. I dare you."

"Um, my psychic abilities aren't really the getting-rid-of-curses kind."

The Jennas exchanged mean little smiles. "Then you're not the real deal," Jenna Jane said, and another murmur rippled through the crowd. This time, it sounded menacing. "If you are, prove it. I. Dare. You."

There was a rushing in Kick's ears. *This so isn't good*, she thought. After all, how could she get rid of something that didn't exist in the first place?

Short answer: She couldn't.

Kick glanced from Natalie May to Mia and, finally, to Cash. Even Carolina had pushed to the crowd's front, and when the cousins' eyes met, Carolina gave her the tiniest head shake. *Don't do it,* her expression said. *Tell the truth!*

Actually, that might not be what Carolina's expression said at all. It's just what Kick assumed. Her cousin could've been saying *Nice knowing you,* but Kick was sure Carolina wanted her to come clean.

And she couldn't. Getting rid of a fake curse with pretend psychic abilities was bad. But admitting she lied and losing her new friends?

That was worse.

"Don't look at *her,*" Jenna Jane snapped, flipping her hair in a way that made her look like she was in a shampoo commercial. "She's probably helping you—"

Carolina gasped. "I would never!"

"Well?" Jenna Jane asked, ignoring her. "What's your answer, *Kick*?"

Honk! Honk!

Everyone whipped around, spotting Carolina's dad—Kick's uncle Freeport—parking his car by the curb. He leaned out the window and waved. "C'mon, girls!"

"Gotta go," Carolina told the crowd, digging her fingers into Kick's arm, and the two of them *ran.*

"There is something approaching on your horizon. I'm not sure if it's good or bad. Ask me again later."

"What's the hurry?" Uncle Freeport asked when Carolina flung the car door open. Carolina didn't answer. She crawled across the bench seat and sat by the far window, leaving her cousin room to climb in after her.

Kick slammed the door and sat back. In terms of exits, that one had been rather unfortunate. Maybe even disastrous.

She eyed Carolina. Matters would definitely turn disastrous if Carolina told Uncle Freeport what happened. Kick took a deep, *deep* breath and prepared to explain the Jennas.

But Carolina said, "No hurry. Just ready to go home."

Her father nodded and put the mint-colored car into drive—or rather, tried to put it in drive. The car stuttered and shuddered and balked. "Easy there, Flubber," Uncle Freeport murmured.

It didn't help. The car only balked more. In Kick's experience, this was to be expected. Uncle Freeport was a former scientist and current mechanic. All of his cars balked or stuttered, or, in one case, belched blue smoke.

Not that her uncle seemed to mind. "Tell me about school," he said, turning up the air-conditioning as if Flubber weren't trying to shake into pieces beneath them. "You two doing okay? It's awfully scary that the Macon twins have disappeared. Do you want to talk about it?"

Flubber lurched forward. Someone behind them honked, and Uncle Freeport waved apologetically. "I heard a whole crowd of folks showed up at your school this morning," he continued. "That must've been something."

Carolina and Kick glanced at each other. It definitely had been something. It'd been a little overwhelming and a little scary, and—okay, maybe more than a little. Stuff was stinking and something was growling and kids were missing. *Missing.*

And Kick was supposed to fix it.

"Everyone was really upset," Carolina said softly. "I've never seen so much yelling."

Uncle Freeport's eyes lifted to the rearview mirror. "Yeah," he said after a beat. "People do that a lot when they're scared."

"Dad, are they going to find the Macon boys?"

There was the smallest of hesitations, and then Uncle

Freeport said, "They're looking for them right now. We're hoping this is another Macon stunt. Those twins are tricksters sometimes."

"They are?" Kick asked.

Her uncle nodded. "Before summer, they put an Open House sign on Miss Sudavee Bark's front yard, and a bunch of people showed up to tour her trailer. It caused a lot of commotion."

Also explains why they thought they were a big deal, Kick thought.

"They've pulled some stunts over the years," he continued. "Carolina can fill you in."

Carolina pursed her lips like she would *not*.

"So they might have disappeared to give everyone a scare?" Kick liked the idea. It was way better than thinking the boys had run off into the swamp and gotten eaten—or transformed or whatever the curse did.

"It could be. Let's not jump to conclusions until we have more facts."

Exactly, Kick thought, snuggling into Flubber's overstuffed cushions. Uncle Freeport drove up the school's lane and turned right to take them out of town and toward the Hollows.

"You okay, Carolina?" His eyes flicked back to the rearview mirror. "You're awfully quiet, honey."

"Long day," Carolina said, and something that sounded

simple suddenly didn't sound so simple at all. Kick wondered about that. Maybe it wasn't any easier being the Girl Who Wears Frilly Dresses than it was being the Girl Who Was Into Science. Sometimes Kick felt like she'd spent her whole life being told what she *couldn't* be, more than what she could.

"I thought that might be the case," Uncle Freeport said, sounding awfully understanding for a grown-up who couldn't possibly know what it was like to endure sixth grade or the Jennas. "Here," he said, passing Carolina something small and slim and square. "I thought this might help."

Help? Kick could use some help. She leaned a little closer and slouched when she saw her uncle had given Carolina a book of fairy tales.

Carolina caught her staring and tucked the book into her bag, and then tucked the bag under her feet. "Thank you."

"I didn't know you liked to read," Kick said, but really she was thinking about the time Carolina had called her chemistry books stupid.

"I do. I just don't like the kind of books you like," Carolina returned, which meant she was also thinking about the time she'd called Kick's chemistry books stupid. "I don't like science. I like real reading."

"You read in science—good stuff too, like directions on how to combine fluids, or how to wash off acids."

"Or blow things up?"

Flubber hit a pothole, and both girls bounced. Uncle Freeport sped past the turnoff for his garage and Kick craned her head, trying to see it. She never could, but it also never stopped her.

They were almost to the Hollows now. The swamp crowded close to the road on both sides, the trees all tangled up with each other. Every time a breeze blew, shadows scattered underneath them.

"I like fairy tales," Carolina added.

"Why? They're not real."

"Fairy tales are plenty real."

"No. They're not." Kick caught her uncle's gaze in the rearview mirror again and expected a fellow scientist to agree with her, but he turned on the radio instead. If it had been music, it might have been rather nice, but Uncle Freeport only listened to people talking, and it was almost as boring as being back in school.

Carolina crossed her arms. "Fairy tales are plenty real. They're like a trapdoor. They take you somewhere else, and you can live a thousand different lives. It's *magic*."

"There's no such thing as magic," Kick said automatically, but now that she thought about it, her cousin might have a point. She loved her chemistry books because she always learned some neat, new detail about the world. It kind of *was* like a trapdoor.

Not that she was inclined to admit it to her cousin.

Uncle Freeport slowed, bringing Flubber to a stop as a fat possum and her baby possums crossed the road. "Easy," he murmured as the mint-colored car's engine rumbled in protest.

"The point is, chemistry is so much—"

Carolina pointed out the window. "Is that what I think it is?"

"What?" Kick looked and looked, seeing nothing and nothing, and then . . . there! On that tree! Was that a smear of glowing green?

It was!

The possums waddled to the other side of the road, and Uncle Freeport started to ease Flubber forward.

"Dad! Look!" Carolina cried.

Uncle Freeport stomped on the brake. Flubber stalled. Smoke crept up from underneath its hood. "Look at wha—"

Kick was already out of the car. She dashed across the road, stopping where the dirt met the grass, and peered into the darkened gap between the swamp trees. It was the end of the shortcut to school.

Where I smelled and heard the monsters, she thought. The memory grabbed her breath. A breeze lifted drooping branches. The Spanish moss swayed. And there it was again! Glowing green!

"Do you see it?" Kick asked as her uncle and cousin climbed out of Flubber.

Uncle Freeport put a hand on Kick's shoulder. This close, she could smell the motor oil on his mechanic's uniform, and when she looked up, she could read his name tag. It said *Miracle Worker*. "Yeah," Uncle Freeport said at last, a grim note stamped in his voice. "I see it."

Kick started forward. "Let's investigate!"

His hand tightened. "Let's not. If the snakes don't get you, the chiggers and leeches will."

Kick slumped. He was right. Still, this was an excellent discovery. "You know what this means, right?"

"It means we're getting back into Flubber and heading for your grandmother's. I brought her groceries, and I don't want them to spoil in the heat."

"But—"

"But nothing. This is a matter for Sheriff Day and Deputy Patel, not us," Uncle Freeport said, steering both girls back to Flubber. He held the door open for them and closed it firmly once they were seated.

"He's right." Carolina watched her father walk around to the driver's side. "If this is some sort of trick, Sheriff Day needs to know."

"Yeah, but so do we. If I can't lift the curse, Jenna Jane will make my life miserable."

Carolina opened her mouth to respond, but Uncle

Freeport climbed in, and she changed her mind. As Flubber lumbered away, Kick twisted around, gripping the back of her seat with both hands.

"Sit down, please," Uncle Freeport asked.

Kick sat. She looked at her cousin, but Carolina ignored her. She looked out the window but didn't see anything glowing. In fact, for the rest of the ride to the Hollows, the swamp looked exactly like it always did.

It should've been disheartening, but Kick couldn't stop her smile. *Bohring Town Curse, my foot,* she thought. Because what came after things that smelled horrible and growls that were terrifying?

Seeing the monsters.

And what self-respecting monster wouldn't glow at night?

None of them, Kick thought, her smile spreading wider and wider. But the thing was, real monsters wouldn't leave glowing smears behind.

But fake monsters and highlighter ink would—so would phosphorescent powder. Or even the stuff inside glow sticks. What was that called again? Phenyl something. It reacted to the hydrogen peroxide inside the glow stick tube.

And then there was bioluminescence. That was usually just in animals, though, wasn't it? It required something. . . .

"Lucifer?" Kick whispered to herself.

The whisper made her uncle go still. "Luci*ferin*," he corrected. "It's required for any chemiluminescence to take place—"

"What?" Carolina asked.

"Chemiluminescence." Uncle Freeport cleared his throat and then cleared it again. "It's the chemical reaction that creates bioluminescence. Like in lightning bugs. Usually, it's because luciferin is reacting to luciferase or photoproteins."

"Oh." Carolina paused. "Looks like glowing paint to me."

"You can make bioluminescent paint from plants," he added. "Although it's not common to find bioluminescent plants. And it's even less common in situations like these."

Which brings us back to highlighter ink, glow sticks, and phenyl-whatever, Kick decided. She waited for her uncle to bring that up, and when he didn't, she did a mental shrug. *Fine, I'll look it up myself.*

And if I can look it up, I can figure it out.

"There is a promise in your future."

When Uncle Freeport and the girls pulled up to the Hollows, a long black limousine was already there. It waited with one tire on the path, dust drifting around the windows like the driver had just squealed up. The right turn signal still flashed.

"Mayor Burr needs some driving lessons," Uncle Freeport said as he angled Flubber well away from the limo's rusted bumper.

Kick thought that was wise. The long black limousine looked like a pothole could shake it apart, and it was inches from poking through Grandma Missouri's equally flimsy fence.

She peered into the darkened windows as they drove past. It was empty inside. "Where's his driver?"

"Fired," her uncle said. "Our mayor thought he could drive himself faster."

"Can he?"

"Well, he certainly can't park any better." Uncle Freeport unfastened his seat belt and got out. The girls followed, and for a moment, there was nothing but the sounds of birds deep in the swamp.

Then came the bellowing.

"It sounds like a cow stuck in a fence," Carolina said.

But it wasn't. It was Mayor Burr. "What do you mean you won't help?" he yelled. "I don't know why, but people listen to you. There's a logical explanation for all of this, and you need to calm them down."

"Or *what*?" Grandma Missouri yelled back.

"C'mon," Uncle Freeport said. "We better get down there or she'll put the eye on him." Before the girls could protest, he strode off toward the Hollows, forcing Carolina and Kick to follow him down the crooked path and over the crooked bridge.

If Grandma Missouri noticed her son-in-law and granddaughters' approach, she didn't act like it. She stood on the Hollows' tilted porch and stared at Mayor Burr like he was a bug and she was a boot.

"No? What do you mean no?" The mayor shook his finger in Grandma Missouri's face and then caught himself. Maybe he'd realized Kick and Carolina and Uncle Freeport were behind him.

Or maybe he'd realized Figgis was floating closer.

The fat alligator drifted slowly under the bridge. Kick knew he was looking for cooler water, but Mayor Burr paled like he was worried Figgis was preparing for a snack.

Burr took a shaky step backward, eyes going from Grandma Missouri to Figgis and back again. "You can't say no. I won't have it."

"Hello, Mayor," Uncle Freeport said. He wasn't facing Kick, but she could hear the easy smile in his voice. "Nice to see you."

"Nice to see you too, Freeport." The mayor jerked his jacket straight and slapped at a mosquito. "Your mother-in-law is being impossible."

Uncle Freeport shrugged. Kick wasn't sure if that meant he agreed or not. Grandma Missouri narrowed her eyes.

The mayor turned to Carolina and Kick. "Hello, girls," he said, sounding larger than he was—or rather, larger than Carolina or Kick, like they were as small to him as they were standing in front of his enormous statue in the center of town.

Grandma Missouri crossed her arms, bangles rattling. "I'm not getting involved with lifting any curses for you, Burr. Now have a good day."

"'Good day'?" The mayor spluttered, his cheeks going redder and redder. Kick couldn't tell if it was because he was so angry or because he was so hot. His dark wool suit was wilted in the damp swamp heat and anyone else would at least take off the jacket, but Grandma Missouri once said Mayor Burr didn't consider himself anyone else.

I wonder how hot it would have to be to make *him take it off,* Kick thought, and then immediately after: *I wonder how hot it would have to be for him to pass out.*

That would be a fun experiment. Not for the mayor obviously, but for Kick it would be fabulous.

"Yes, have a good day," Grandma Missouri said, deepening her voice, "and may the devil always be confused on the way to your home."

Mayor Burr swung his head from side to side. He looked at Uncle Freeport (who looked at the tree branches overhead) and looked back at Grandma Missouri (who looked straight at him). He had no idea what was going on. Kick felt a tiny bit bad for him. She didn't understand her grandmother half the time either.

"I'll remember this!" Mayor Burr promised. He spun on his shiny shoe's heel and stalked up the path toward the cars, gnats swirling around his pink bald spot. Grandma Missouri made the disgusted noise she reserved for people who telephoned during dinner. Then she stalked inside the Hollows and slammed the door with a hard *whump!*

The girls flinched. Figgis ducked under the water. "I've never seen the mayor so mad," Carolina whispered, watching him stomp around the limousine. He climbed in the front seat and jerked the door shut. The long black limousine flew backward and then lurched forward, throwing dust into the air, bits of gravel spitting from beneath its tires.

"Why is he so mad at Grandma Missouri for not wanting to get involved?" Kick asked.

Her uncle considered this. "Probably because he had to ask her for a favor and she turned him down. They've never gotten along. He thinks she takes people's money and tells them what they want to hear."

"Why would that make him mad?" Carolina asked.

"Politicians don't like the competition."

"Huh?" the girls said in unison.

"Never mind. Forget I said anything. This is what we're going to do: Carolina, why don't you go in and say hi to your grandma?"

Carolina's mouth wadded up. Kick knew her cousin didn't want to go in there—Grandma Missouri was difficult when annoyed—but Carolina went anyway, trudging into the Hollows like she had no choice.

Why did grown-ups think because they *asked* someone to do something, it wasn't the same as *ordering* someone to do something? The ingredients might be different, but the result was identical.

Need to write that one down too, Kick thought.

"And you," Uncle Freeport said, turning to his niece, "you can help me with the groceries, okay?"

Kick nodded, following him up the path to Flubber. Uncle Freeport took out two brown paper bags of fresh vegetables and frozen waffles. Thanks to being in the trunk, they were more like soggy waffles.

Kick waited while Uncle Freeport gathered up potatoes that had escaped their bag and rolled into the trunk's corners. Now that the mayor was gone, she'd had time to think and all she could think about was Jenna Jane, the curse, and that glowing smear.

"Uncle Freeport?"

He didn't answer, but Kick knew from the way he tilted his head that he was listening.

"What do you know about the curse?"

He straightened, a pockmarked potato in each hand. "Every hundred years—"

"I know *that.*" She paused, almost disappointed in herself that she was about to ask: "Do you believe in it?"

"Sort of." Uncle Freeport dropped the potatoes into the bag. "People used to think the world was flat. They thought they had it all figured out, and then someone—"

"Pythagoras, but maybe other philosophers too—"

"And then *someone* came along and proved everyone wrong. Nowadays, we still think we have it all figured out, but I'm not convinced we do. Doesn't mean I believe in curses necessarily, but I do believe people can be monsters, and they can make more than enough trouble for other folks. They might even have made the kind of trouble that involves the glow we saw in the swamp. Make sense?"

Kick nodded.

"Anyway," her uncle added, hoisting the bags of groceries into his arms, "whether we believe in the curse or not is immaterial. Everyone *else* believes in the curse, and they'd rather blame that than admit something more logical—and maybe even more dangerous—is happening."

"So you don't believe in curses, but you *do* believe something's going on?"

Uncle Freeport considered her for so long—and in such horrible silence—Kick was convinced he was going to shush her and never answer. "Something is *definitely* going on in Bohring," he said finally, "and whatever it is, I want you and Carolina to stay out of it."

Excitement surged through her. Uncle Freeport knew the curse wasn't adding up too! She wasn't the only person who saw it!

He glowered at her. "I'm not kidding. Do you understand?"

"Yes," she said because she did understand. She also understood it didn't help her Jenna Jane situation. At *all*.

Time to get inventive.

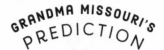

"You're going to fail. How you react to that failure is up to you."

But, hours later, Kick still didn't have a plan. She lay under her covers and fumed. The longer she thought about how she needed a good idea, the less her brain wanted to cooperate.

Hmmm. Was that experiment book-worthy? She wasn't sure. She wrote it down anyway:

Wednesday, September 11, 12:02 a.m.
Hypothesis: If I need to get Jenna Jane to leave me alone,
then my brain shrivels up and refuses to help me.

Kick scowled. It *did* seem like the data would support such an assumption. Still scowling, she flung the bedcovers off her legs and peeked out the window. Moonlight edged fallen trees and turned the water silver. Everything looked precisely as it should.

Kick pressed her cheek to the window, trying to see up the crooked path toward the road. Useless. She was too far away.

But she couldn't stop thinking about that glowing green smear.

It wasn't *that* far. Maybe a two-minute walk?

If it's still there, Kick thought, using the edge of her T-shirt to scrub her face print off the window glass.

Below, the yellow lights of the kitchen snapped off. Grandma Missouri was heading to bed, and Kick felt a sudden tingling in her fingertips. She scrubbed a little harder at the window. Sometimes, tingling meant her fingers were tired, but most of the time, tingling meant she had an idea.

A really good idea.

I should go find that glowing smear. She studied her shadowy reflection in the clean window and decided it definitely was one of her better ideas.

Even if it was also her scariest.

Going out in the *dark*? In the *swamp*? She opened her window a crack and then a bit more. Swamp sounds and swamp smells climbed through: the splash of water, the scent of rot, the rustle of Figgis.

Goose bumps prickled her arms. It was one thing to admire the alligator from behind the porch railing. It was quite another to go wandering past his space in the dark.

With the snakes.

And the spiders.

And the—

How bad do you want to know what that glow is? Kick asked herself, which helped. A bit. *How bad do you want to prove the curse is fake?*

Which helped quite a bit more.

If she figured out the glow, she could figure out the curse, and *then* she could figure out how to lift it.

And no one would ever know she'd lied about being psychic. Jenna Jane would never be able to mess with her again. She'd probably be a town hero—maybe she'd give a speech on how she lifted the curse.

Just like Mom, Kick thought, reaching for her coveralls and sneakers. *Well, sort of like Mom.* Dr. Georgia Winter gave lectures on scientific discoveries. Kick would be lecturing on *psychic* discoveries, but whatever.

She still couldn't bring herself to climb out the window. All her thoughts hinged on what was waiting for her in the dark. Like hungry alligators or monsters or the *twins.*

Exactly, she reminded herself. *If I'm scared, imagine how they feel.* Not to mention she was the last person who saw them.

It makes you responsible. It was her father's voice and it came from inside her head, but it was still clear as day. Like it or not, she was involved and she couldn't turn away.

It wasn't the most comforting realization, but it did force her to ease one foot out the window—and then the other. Holding her breath, Kick went from the window to the roof, from the roof to the bare rose trellis, and from the bare rose trellis to the porch. When her sneakers hit the peeling porch floorboards, her breath left her. She'd done it. She was outside.

Alone.

At *night*.

She shook herself. *How bad do you want to prove the curse is fake? How bad do you want to help the Macon boys?*

Again, it helped. She moved one frozen foot forward and then the other, tiptoeing past the front door and down the front steps. She ran across the crooked bridge and up the crooked path, glancing back one last time to make sure the Hollows' windows were still dark.

Everyone in Bohring thought the cottage was terrifying—well, except for Mayor Burr, who said it was unsanitary.

Right now, the Hollows looked rather pretty peeking through the trees. Paper lanterns swayed in the damp breeze and the colored Christmas lights turned its clapboard siding red, green, and purple.

The image centered Kick—not that she knew it. She only knew her chest loosened, and it was suddenly easier to go on because the Hollows was right behind her, waiting. The dark was just the dark. The swamp was still the swamp. She could do this.

She stuck to the edge of the dusty dirt road, long grass whipping around her legs, and walked.

And walked.

And *walked*.

Kick frowned. How far had she come? It felt like she should've reached the glow.

Did I miss it? she wondered, retracing her steps. *Or is it gone?*

Did someone clean it up?

Was it taken into evidence by Sheriff Day?

Above, the sky was clogged with trembling stars, and the full moon dipped everything in silver and black. Crickets chirped. Something splashed.

Something rustled.

Kick tripped. She leaped out of the long grass and stood in the middle of the road, listening. Something rustled again.

The night felt closer, thicker. The dark wasn't just the dark. It was a breathing, waiting, *listening* dark. The wind picked up, making the swamp shadows twitch. She could smell wet pines and wetter earth and—

Something foul.

Kick froze as the woods went quiet. No birds cried out. No bugs hummed in the long grass. Near the water's edge, something exhaled.

She took a step back, legs shaking. Her nose filled with a stench and her head filled with a schoolyard rhyme: *One, two, monsters coming for you! Three, four, they're outside your door! Five, six, first it smells like Styx! Seven, eight, hear the growls of fate! Nine, ten, see the monsters again!*

"It's not monsters," she breathed, forcing her legs to work, her feet to move. "It's just the swamp."

But she knew it wasn't. She knew it was just like before when she'd smelled the smell and then heard the growl and—

Splash!

It came from behind her. Kick whirled around. There was only the dusty road and the overgrown swamp. She was alone.

Splash!

She whirled again, eyes hunting the shadows clotted underneath the trees, the spiky stumps reaching up from the water, the glimmer glow of something just beyond a swaying willow. Something was in there, something like—

"*Lights,*" she whispered. Lights were weaving toward her, faintly green under the trees' shadows. "Swamp gas."

It *had* to be swamp gas. Just like the mayor said, there was a reasonable explanation for all of this, and it didn't get much more reasonable than the scientific effect of all those rotting trees and leaves creating . . .

What was that stuff again?

Methane!

Kick felt her knees go steadier. Yes, methane. "Methane

reacts with the phosphines in the air and results in swamp lights," she recited, pulling the words from memory. Each one made her feel less shaky. Scientists weren't supposed to get scared. They were supposed to figure things out.

"Swamp gas," Kick repeated as the lights bounced closer. She stopped, that foul stench swirling around her. It smelled like mall bathrooms and roadkill. Kick might have felt queasy if she'd been paying attention, but she wasn't. She was too busy studying the lights.

When did swamp gas start bouncing? she wondered, but she didn't get to wonder it for long because the lights weren't lights at all. They were *figures*, and the figures weren't just figures, they were *horrible* figures.

Low to the ground with four legs and smashed-in faces, they splashed through the shallow water, leaped over fallen branches. Shaggy, muddy hair whipped around their wrinkled snouts. Every breath was a snarl.

Yes, indeed, they were horrible, and they were glowing, and they were green—one might even say *monster* green, but Kick wouldn't because she was already running.

Gogogo!

She ran ten strides . . . twenty . . . before she dared a glance over her shoulder, spotting the glowing green headed in the opposite direction.

The monsters weren't chasing her at all.

They were headed for *Bohring*.

"Another opportunity is coming your way."

"It's like déjà vu all over again," Kick muttered later that morning—because just like yesterday, the schoolyard was packed with angry grown-ups. Just like yesterday, Dr. Callahan looked nervous and Mr. Grimp was sporting suspiciously stained overalls.

And just like yesterday, Mayor Burr was yelling from the steps. "People! Whatever you think you saw last night, you didn't! I'm your mayor, and I'm telling you this is impossible! You have to trust me! I'm asking you to listen!"

They didn't, of course. The crowd's murmurs had a beehive hum. Everywhere Kick looked, anxious grown-ups looked back. Even Deputy Patel was frazzled, pieces of wavy black hair escaping her usually smooth braid. Her uniform was rumpled like she'd slept in it.

She probably did, Kick realized. She'd probably been up all night searching for the Macon boys. The mayor wasn't much better. His comb-over stood up in spikes, his shirt was half-untucked, and the more he yelled, the more the whites of his eyes showed. "I'm on top of this!" he bellowed. "When have I ever let you down?"

"Oh, please!" Miss Ruth tried to step forward, but two other women held her back. "This is bigger than kissing babies and dedicating benches to town council members. This is the *curse*, Burr! My boys are *missing*!"

The crowd shifted and rumbled. Gritting her teeth, Kick edged into it, looking for Natalie May and Mia.

"First off, Miss Ruth," Mayor Burr said, hand pinned to his heart—or his Vote for Burr button, "I am doing every-thing in my power to bring your boys home safely." He paused, and a smattering of applause rippled through the crowd. Satisfied, he continued on. "Secondly, Sheriff Day, Deputy Patel, and I are looking into who could be behind this vicious growling prank. It will *not* be tolerated."

Makes him sound like a hero, Kick thought, rubbing her eyes. They felt gritty and itchy, and all she wanted to do was lie down and take a nap. Nighttime searches definitely had their drawbacks come morning. She slipped around Mr. Grimp and spotted Mia standing by the swing set. Mia looked up, spotting her too, and waved her closer.

Miss Ruth spit into the dirt. "We need to handle this ourselves!" she yelled to the crowd. "Our children are on the line, and we need to be on the lookout!"

Roar went the crowd. Or at least that's what it sounded like. Kick cringed as everyone began shouting at once. She shouldered her way to Mia, who grabbed her hand, chilled fingers tightening around Kick's own.

"With all due respect, Miss Ruth," the mayor said, "what happened last night was a prank, and before we start accusing people of not doing their jobs, perhaps we should consider whose children are known for, ahem, their sense of *humor.*"

Miss Ruth's gasp rode over the crowd. "How dare you! My boys are *missing*! They couldn't have anything to do with glowing monsters!"

"Maybe they're pretending to be missing," Mayor Burr said.

There was another gasp from Miss Ruth, but Kick caught herself wanting to nod. She didn't know anything about the twins' "sense of humor," but pranks made a lot more sense than monsters.

Except for the fact that you saw *the monsters too,* she thought, frowning.

"If the curse is coming true," Mia whispered, "we could be *next.*"

"There's no such thing as curses," Kick told her, and she might have said it with a little too much force because people ahead of them turned around.

"Oh, yeah?" A woman propped one hand on her hip.

"If there's no curse, then how do you explain the monsters? Because I saw 'em last night. My brother's saw 'em too. Tell 'em, Earl!"

Earl nodded. "I saw 'em."

"See?" the woman said.

No, Kick thought as she studied the grown-ups. They looked almost exactly alike—same black hair, same UGA football jersey—but where the man wore his whiskers on his cheeks, the woman wore them on her eyebrows, and when she squinted down at Kick, those whiskery eyebrows nearly met over her nose.

"I saw those monsters clear as I see you now," she said. "What do you say to that?"

Well, technically, Kick couldn't say anything. She'd seen them clearly too.

"That's what I thought," the woman said.

"C'mon, Jolene!" someone cried. "Give it up!"

Jolene glared at the crowd. "This isn't just about Buford and Buddy! Earl could've been attacked! Those monsters were glowing and running through that swamp like they were *born* from it!"

The crowd fell silent. Mayor Burr and Miss Ruth fell silent. Jolene nodded grimly. "I mean, come on, people— those things were *green!*"

"So that makes them monsters?" Kick asked, keeping her voice sweet and face blank just like she did when she swore to Grandma Missouri she wouldn't experiment anymore. "Because aliens are green too. Or *maybe* we're dealing with swamp gas that makes stuff look green. It could be an aberration—"

"The little girl is right!" Mayor Burr yelled.

"Who's he calling 'little girl'?" Kick demanded.

"I think you might want to be quiet now." Mia tugged Kick tight against her side, both hands covering her mouth. "That stuff about aliens is crazy talk."

True—but so was the monster talk . . . and so was the grown-ups' talk. They were arguing again. The air around Kick had a hair-raising energy. It made her teeth itch.

"Everyone settle down!" Deputy Patel yelled at the crowd. "We have questions for all of you, and we need you to be *calm!*"

"Thank you, Deputy," Mayor Burr said, face bright red. "Good citizens of Bohring, I have this under control!"

But the good citizens of Bohring erupted like they didn't believe him at all.

"See? I told you, it's the curse— and that'll be five dollars. We take cash, check, money order, or trade."

Kick was disappointed to report the day was pretty much downhill from there. It shouldn't have been. Being questioned by Deputy Patel about what happened in the swamp should've been thrilling. But telling the truth—"We smelled this awful stench and something was growling in the swamp and the twins took off"—actually didn't sound like the truth at all.

And Kick could tell Deputy Patel thought she was making the whole thing up.

"You're Grandma Missouri's granddaughter, aren't you?" she asked, brown eyes still on her notepad.

"Yes."

"Got it." But it sounded more like: *That explains the story.* "I'll let you know if I have any follow-up questions. Can you send in the next student?"

Kick did, thinking this was pretty pointless—and class

wasn't any better. No one could concentrate. The Jennas kept whispering, Cash kept twitching, and Mrs. Flagg's grip on her whiteboard marker seemed to be especially tight.

"In many ways, Bohring has a common-enough past: We have a shameful history of segregation and oppression.

"But," Mrs. Flagg continued, "we have also been the subject of some notoriety—"

"What?" Jefferson asked.

"Being known for something that makes people give you side-eye," Mia said.

Mrs. Flagg's grip tightened even more. "That's one way of putting it. But Bohring is also known in psychology circles as being an example of collective hysteria or mass hysteria after several townspeople reported smelling and hearing things a hundred years ago."

"Maybe they really *were* smelling and hearing things," Cash said.

"Or maybe they were imagining it," Mrs. Flagg countered.

Exactly, Kick thought—although it meant she'd imagined smelling and hearing stuff just yesterday. It was annoying.

"So, in summary," Mrs. Flagg continued, "Bohring has a wealth of history for you to explore in your projects, and I hope you'll remember to use our very own Bohring Town Historical Society during your research."

She smiled at the class. The class stared back until her smile faltered. Normally, Kick would feel terrible about this. Mrs. Flagg was lovely and kind and deserved students who were excited, but it was difficult enough to be excited about a history project on the best of days, and today was certainly *not* the best of days.

"Speaking of history projects," Mrs. Flagg added, her faltering smile faltering even more, "who would like to talk about theirs? Jefferson? Where are you on your project?"

"Deep in the thick of it, Mrs. Flagg."

"'Deep in the thick of it' *how*? Can you explain it to us?"

Jefferson could not, and Kick knew it even before he opened his mouth. She looked down at her history book, and someone kicked her desk.

It was Jenna H. She smirked and nodded her head to the right.

Toward Jenna Jane.

"What?" Kick mouthed.

"Made your decision yet?" Jenna Jane whispered.

Kick frowned. There were a lot of answers she could pick from here. Of *course* Jenna Jane meant *Have you made your decision about lifting the curse?* but since she hadn't been specific, Kick could play dumb and go with *Decision about what?* Or play aloof and go with *I make so many decisions, to which are you referring?*

"No talking in class, ladies," Mrs. Flagg snapped, attention still trained on Jefferson.

Jenna Jane faced the whiteboard, and Kick went back to her notebook, doodling loops in the margins and puzzling through possible swamp gas aberrations.

Which was rather a shame because she entirely missed when Cash leaped to his feet, flailing.

"It won't leave me alone!" he yelped. "It won't stop buzzing!"

Kick jumped, watching as Cash shrieked and pawed his forehead—definitely his eyebrow. "Make it stop!" he yelled.

Make what stop? As far as Kick could tell, nothing was buzzing. The air was, well, *air*.

Mrs. Flagg surged toward Cash as he spun in another circle. "I'm not a monster!" he shouted at her. "Tell it I'm not a monster!"

"What are you talking about?" Mrs. Flagg grabbed for Cash's hands. Cash danced out of reach. "What's going on?"

He tugged at his hair. "I'm not next! Make the voices stop!"

"Make *what* voices stop?"

"You don't hear that?"

"Hear *what*?" Mrs. Flagg tried to hold his shoulders. "I don't hear anything. You're being—"

"Ugh!" Cash hurled himself over Jenna B.'s desk. She screamed. Mrs. Flagg shrieked. Cash didn't stop. He skidded out the door and pounded down the hallway.

"Cash!" Mrs. Flagg took off after him. At the doorway, she turned to the class, jamming one finger at them. "Do. Not. Move." Then she ran.

No one said anything.

The air conditioner kicked on. The ceiling mobiles began to spiral. Then Jefferson Burr spoke up: "Well, you know what this means, the curse has begun and we're all doomed. Now, who wants to buy a lucky penny?"

Everyone's hands shot into the air.

Well, everyone's except for Kick's. She was too busy thinking—not so busy thinking that she didn't notice Carolina's hand wasn't in the air either, though. The girls looked at each other and then looked away.

This curse stuff doesn't make sense, Kick thought, which honestly was not a new thought, but suddenly it felt new and she didn't understand why.

Then she did.

"He'd been hearing things for a while," she breathed. It was Wednesday, but Cash had asked her on *Monday* if she had heard anything.

"What?" Mia snatched a glance in Kick's direction, brows knotted. "Did you say something?"

"Nothing. It's . . . nothing." But it wasn't, and the more Kick thought about it, the more she knew it was most certainly *something*. How did the rhyme go? *Five, six, first it smells like Styx! Seven, eight, hear the growls of fate!*

First you smelled the smell. *Then* you heard the growls.

Kick sat up straight. *It's out of order,* she realized. Just like in chemistry, there was a procedure to the curse, and the voices Cash had heard didn't fit the procedure. Not only were they out of order, but they weren't supposed to be *voices.*

An aberration, Kick thought, watching the other students clamber to Jefferson's side. They elbowed each other out of the way, desperate to get lucky pennies into their hands.

The monsters had been glowing, Cash had heard voices, and now Kick was stuck.

Or was she?

Maybe I'm going about this all wrong, she thought, turning to study Cash's desk. Nothing seemed out of place. The afternoon sun poured through the window, yellow and generous as butter on warm toast.

Maybe I don't need to find what's glowing or smelling, she thought, feeling her fingers begin to tingle. *Maybe I just need to find what was . . . talking.*

"An unexpected ally will come to your rescue."

Thursday, September 12, 7:00 a.m.
Best Plan Ever
Observation: Something is going on in Mrs. Flagg's classroom.
Procedure to collect data:
Get into classroom alone. Investigate.
Procedure to get into classroom alone: a distraction.
Distraction possibilities:
use Figgis's chicken cutlets as stink bomb,
tell Mrs. Flagg the spirits would like her to step outside for a bit,
(smoke)
Procedure to create smoke: pour mineral oil
onto hot Bunsen burner.

And when Mrs. Flagg left her classroom to investigate the smoke distraction, Kick would slip in and perform her research. It was simple, effective. Indeed, it *was* her best plan ever.

If she could get it to work.

Kick dragged dirty clothes away from her closet and hauled the door open. She lifted up one box of taxidermied squirrels and then another box of taxidermied-squirrel clothes. *No . . . no . . . no . . . there it is!* The burner was buried underneath a knot of old fishing line and older *Scientific American* magazines.

Kick crammed it into her book bag, shoved the clothes back in front of the closet door, and fluffed socks until everything looked precisely messy enough.

Now for the mineral oil.

Thankfully, that part was easy since Grandma Missouri always kept a bottle under the sink. Kick added it to her book bag, left a note about going into school early, and tiptoed out the front door feeling extremely pleased with herself.

Or she was until she spotted a figure coming up the road.

Kick squinted. The figure was fluffy . . . and white . . . and—the figure was Carolina.

Today, her cousin wore a smocked white dress with lacy white socks and salmon-pink shoes. Her hair was woven into two plaits. They bounced angrily as Carolina stomped toward Kick. "Where do you think you're going?"

"School."

"Why so early?"

"I'm a go-getter." Kick's eyes dipped, snagging on the

fluffy white dress's collar. Were those . . . embroidered bumblebees? They *were*.

"What are you looking at?"

"Nothing. You look very nice."

"I'm serious. What are you up to?"

"School." Kick squared her shoulders. "Why are *you* here so early?"

"Because of yesterday. I know you're going to do something outrageous. You can't tell Jenna Jane you're a fraud, so you're going to escalate. I know you. I know how you think."

Kick paused. "You're a very suspicious person, you know that?"

Carolina's eyes bugged. "You're going to make it worse for *both* of us. Trust me, you don't want to mess with that girl. She's mean."

"I noticed." This early, pink and gold edged the treetops, and in the swamp, birds were singing. It was quite picturesque—if you could ignore the mosquitoes, which Kick couldn't. She slapped at one as Carolina glared at her.

"I'm not leaving," she said.

"Fine."

"Fine." Neither of them moved. Carolina lowered her chin. "If you don't stop, Jenna Jane is going to make us both miserable."

Kick looked at Carolina.

Carolina looked at Kick.

She really isn't going anywhere, Kick realized. "*Or* you could help me out, and we'd both be free of her."

"*What?*"

"I need to get into Mrs. Flagg's room to find out what was talking to Cash."

Carolina made a very unladylike snort, or maybe it only seemed very unladylike because she was dressed like Princess Posey Getting Married.

"Before you freak out," Kick told her, "think about it: The curse has a procedure. First you smell the smell, then you hear the growls, *then* you see the monsters and turn into one. But Cash was hearing something *before* the smell. It's out of order."

Carolina paused, her brown eyes going suddenly bright. "I didn't know he'd heard something before."

"He asked me about it on Monday. It's an aberration, and if you knew anything about science, you'd know—"

"That it's worth investigating."

Kick deflated.

"What? You're not the only one with a scientist parent."

"Whatever, if we can figure out what happened to Cash, we can lift the curse and get Jenna Jane to leave *both* of us alone."

Carolina chewed her lower lip. "Okay, but how are you going to get Mrs. Flagg to leave?"

Kick held out her backpack, and her cousin peeked inside. "I don't get it."

"I'm going to pour mineral oil on the Bunsen burner. It'll smoke."

Carolina's mouth hung open. *"That's* your plan?"

"It's a distraction."

"It's vandalism. You could cause smoke damage."

Carolina had a point.

"How are you going to keep from getting caught?" her cousin asked.

"I'm not sure. It's a work in progress."

Carolina opened her mouth, closed it, and then opened it again. "Where are you going to put it?"

"Teachers' bathroom."

"No way." A swampy breeze swirled around the girls, and Carolina's braids twitched like they'd come alive. "If you put it in the bathroom, you'll set off the fire alarms and you won't be able to search because they'll evacuate the school."

Another good point. Kick frowned.

"How long before the mineral oil smokes?" Carolina finally asked.

"I don't know. Couple of minutes probably."

"You can fit a lifetime of grounding into 'probably.' You need to beta test it."

"Since when do you know anything about beta—"

"C'mon. We need to do this now, and I have a cat to feed." Carolina spun around, white skirt lifting like a sail, and after the briefest of hesitations, Kick followed.

"Nothing is as it seems."

Carolina, Kick decided several minutes later, *has been holding out on me.* Not only did her cousin know about beta testing— a fantastically important-sounding way to describe testing a product or in this case a distraction—but she also had a laboratory.

Or rather, she had Zora Lee's bungalow.

The bungalow, squat and painted an infected pink, was Grandma Missouri's closest neighbor. Swamp leaked around its cinder-block supports, and bugs circled the porch lights.

Carolina went to the equally pink front door and tugged a key from her backpack. She unlocked the door and motioned Kick inside. "Don't touch anything. Don't look at anything. Don't even breathe on anything."

"What if I cough?"

"What if you don't?"

Inside, the bungalow was dim, crowded with furniture and collectibles. Everywhere Kick looked, tiny cherubs with enormous eyes looked back. She was pretty sure they were supposed to be cute. They weren't. Their enormous eyes were closer to agonized than adorable.

Kick took a deep breath, smelling air that was musty, dusty, and overfull.

Suspiciously overfull, now that she thought about it.

Like something was waiting.

"This doesn't feel righ— Ahhh!" A furry missile exploded from the musty, dusty dark and attached itself to Kick's ankles. She hopped around, batting at it, but the bats only made the missile angrier. It bit down harder, a silky tail now wrapping around the claws and teeth.

"Awww." Carolina smirked. "He loves you."

Kick shook her leg, trying (unsuccessfully) to dislodge an enormous cat from her shin. "You could've said something!"

"But it would've ruined the surprise. Kick, meet Catsanova. Catsanova, meet Kick."

Catsanova released Kick's leg so he could bare his teeth and hiss.

Kick hissed back. "He's enormous," she told Carolina.

Carolina shrugged.

Catsanova hissed again. "And we're here because . . . ?" Kick asked.

"I have to feed him."

"Feed him what? Small children?"

"Cat food. Miss Zora is visiting her sister and asked me to take care of him. That thing of yours needs electricity to work, right?"

It took Kick a full thirty seconds to figure Carolina was talking about her Bunsen burner. "It does."

"Then this is a perfect laboratory. Ms. Zora thinks smoke detectors are spies for the government."

Normally, Kick would've sighed. She might have even counted to ten for patience. She *definitely* would've added a comment about how ridiculous Ms. Zora was. But right now? Right now, that was about the best thing she'd ever heard. "Let's do this."

Carolina hoisted Catsanova into her arms, and they both eyed Kick with suspicion. "You're *positive* this won't burn down her house?"

"Almost entirely."

Carolina took a deep breath and then another. "I'm envisioning a future with no Jennas," she muttered, dragging the cat down the hallway and, presumably, toward the kitchen for breakfast.

Kick watched her go. She too was envisioning a future with no Jennas, but she was also envisioning a future with an extremely effective smoke bomb. She glanced at the white-faced clock above Ms. Zora's television. They had roughly twenty minutes to experiment.

Slinging off her backpack, Kick unzipped the top and pulled out the Bunsen burner. It was rather a shame to experiment with it like this. She'd had plans for the burner: the boiling kind, obviously, but also an occasional grilled cheese sandwich. What if the oil ruined it?

Sometimes sacrifices have to be made, Kick reminded herself. *Plus, it's for the good of the town.* She set the burner down on the orange shag carpeting, plugged the cord into the closest socket, and pulled out her mineral oil. It swirled clear and thick behind the plastic.

"Now or never." She dumped a dollop onto the burner's ceramic plate and then, when that didn't seem like enough, dumped a dollop more. "Let's see how that goes."

It didn't take long.

The burner began to spit and then hiss. Tendrils of smoke began to reach for the water-stained ceiling. It was a nice effect.

But not enough to attract teachers, Kick thought, upending the bottle as her cousin came back down the hallway. And maybe it was the increasing heat or maybe it was the increasing mineral oil.

Or maybe it was Carolina's appearance.

But black-gray smoke began to blossom in earnest, and Kick couldn't stop her smile. "Totally works," she said, waving one hand in front of her face.

"No joke." Carolina bent down, yanking the burner's

plug from the outlet. She did it with such force the faded family pictures hanging on the wall trembled in their frames. "Help me open the windows."

"Why? Introducing a new element will affect the experiment."

Carolina shot her such a dark look, Kick suddenly realized the point. "Oh. Right."

Letting Ms. Zora come back to a stinky house wasn't exactly neighborly. Not to mention it wasn't exactly subtle. If Ms. Zora came home and smelled something weird, she'd call Aunt Aly, who would probably call Grandma Missouri, who would *definitely* suspect Kick of being up to something.

Carolina took the window by the television stand, and Kick took the one by a shelf of cherubs. They wrenched the windows open. Fresh, humid air spilled in, the cherubs reemerged, and the acrid smell began to dissipate.

Carolina took a step back, watching the smoke drift away. She stood in a wedge of sunlight, and the dust motes turned gold around her. "I can't believe I'm doing this."

Honestly? Kick couldn't either. "Think of yourself like a reaction. You know when potassium is combined with water and you get an explosion?"

"No."

"Oh. Well, pretend you're that. You might not be someone who normally explodes, but you are when you're combined with me."

Carolina's mouth pressed into a flat line. "How about if I pretend I'm Princess Posey and I'm saving my kingdom?"

"Whatever you need to tell yourself."

Even though the burner had been unplugged, the smoke still curled around and around the ceiling, turning everything hazy.

Suspicious, Kick thought, satisfied. There was no way a teacher would see this kind of smoke and *not* investigate.

"A huge success," she decided, waving one hand in front of her face. It didn't do much good. Even with the open window, her eyes still burned. "It's totally going to work."

"Yeah, it is."

Catsanova strutted down the hallway and into the living room. He hissed. "I know, right?" Kick asked him. The cat scurried off. "This was really great, Carolina. Thanks."

"You're welcome."

"I need a laboratory." Kick rocked back and forth on her heels, trying to decide if the cherubs' presence lessened the discovery, because it kind of felt like they did. "A proper one. Not a closet or someone's house."

"Yeah."

It was one word, but there was something about the way the word lifted that made Kick turn. She studied her cousin, and her cousin suddenly studied her shoes.

Such pink shoes, Kick thought. "Carolina?"

"What?"

"I've got to ask . . . what's with the dresses?"

"What's *what* with the dresses?"

"You know."

"My mom likes them," she said at last.

"I know. But do you?"

"That isn't the point."

Kick thought about it. "It isn't?"

"You've never done something to make your parents happy?"

"Okay, fine, you got me there, but why don't you have any friends?"

Carolina winced. "I don't know. People are really nice around here—well, except for the Jennas—but I get nervous talking to them."

"You're never nervous talking to me."

"You're not people." Her cousin sighed. "You don't get it. You've lived all over the place, so you're used to making yourself fit in."

"But you can't?"

Carolina pointed at the bumblebees. "What do you think?"

"I think you should own it, and if you do that hard enough, the right friends will find you."

Frowning, Carolina glanced at her watch. "We don't have time to set the smoke distraction up today; it's cutting things too close. But Friday for sure."

"Really? Because it'll only take a few minutes at most and—"

"Do I look like someone who's kidding?"

Kick thought it over. She looked from the embroidered bumblebees to the fluffy skirt to the prissy shoes. "No?"

Carolina's expression turned suspicious. "I can't tell if you're being serious."

"I'm being serious, and you're right. Timing is crucial with this. We don't want to risk being spotted."

Her cousin's breath whooshed out of her. "Exactly. Now, see? Was that really so hard? You're just like Grandma Missouri. Mom says she's always flying off the handle and saying things she shouldn't. If you'd just take a few extra minutes to think things through, you wouldn't be in this mess."

"Oh, yeah? How many people in Bohring are thinking through the curse?"

Carolina frowned.

"That's right. None of them. But *I* am." Kick groped around in her book bag until she found her experiment notebook. She opened it to the first page. "Let's make it official. If monsters are real, then I'll prove it," she said, writing down her premise in big letters.

Then (in even bigger letters) she added to the top of the page:

The Monster Hypothesis

"People can be surprising— not to me, of course, but to you."

As promised, Carolina met Kick early on Friday morning. The air was almost cool, and walking through the shortcut, they could hear a search party in the distance, calling for Buddy and Buford.

Kick shivered. "Think they'll find them?"

"Of course they will." But Carolina didn't sound like she believed it. "You have the stuff?"

"You mean my Bunsen burner, mineral oil, and glorious plan?"

"I cannot with you today. I cannot." Carolina sped up, hands fisted at her sides.

So touchy, Kick thought, but she also sped up. All the grown-ups calling in the distance was creepy. *Or maybe the swamp is always creepy.*

It was quite the conundrum, one that kept Kick busy all the way to school and then all the way around to the back of the school and *then* all the way to just outside Miss Welty's window.

"Plug it in," Carolina instructed, looking down at the socket wedged between bricks. "Let's do this."

Kick did. It took a few minutes for the burner to warm, and then she squeezed the whole bottle of mineral oil onto the plate. "Run for it!"

Carolina grabbed her hand. "This way."

She led them back the way they came, toward the tiny black door that was the school's sole rear entrance. Carolina yanked it open.

"Janitor's closet," she hissed, pointing to their right. It was *another* tiny black door. Kick ducked inside, and Carolina jerked the door shut behind them.

At first, there was only darkness. Then Kick's eyes adjusted. Light leaked around the doorframe, illuminating the cramped space just enough that she *would have* looked at her cousin in new admiration. But she couldn't, since she was wedged between two shelves of cleaning solutions and ever so slightly worried she would never get back out. "How did you know the janitor's closet would be open?"

"You think you're the first girl Jenna Jane had bullied? I've been hiding in here for *years*." A moment passed and then another—then footsteps pounded past. Carolina leaned closer to the closet's keyhole, watching the teachers rush by and not even flinching.

In spite of herself, Kick was impressed. Her cousin had increasing potential. "You know," she whispered, shifting around to get more comfortable, "I'm kind of upset we didn't get to the see the smoke—"

"I'm not. Stop fidgeting. You'll get us caught for sure."

Kick had no idea how trying to give herself enough room to breathe would get them caught, but it wasn't worth arguing over. Carefully, she nudged the bottle of bleach to one side and rested her chin on the shelf. It put her at eye level with more bottles of bleach and a clear glass jar filled with clear thin liquid.

To keep herself distracted, Kick slid her index finger behind the glass, several inches away from the liquid. She watched as her finger appeared from the opposite side of the glass. If things had been less tense, she would've explained light refraction to Carolina.

She also would've wondered why the clear liquid smelled a bit like turpentine.

"They're gone." Carolina eased open the door and slipped into the hallway. After a tiny struggle to unwedge herself, Kick crept after her, positive her sneakers had never sounded so loud.

Carolina peeked inside Mrs. Flagg's classroom. "It's empty. Hurry up."

Kick hurried. "You check the walls, the heating vents." She rubbed clammy hands along her coveralls, glancing around the empty classroom. This suddenly didn't seem like such a good idea. "I'll start with Cash's desk. Someone must've hidden something somewhere."

"Someone hid something somewhere?"

She pushed Carolina toward the other side of the room. "Just look around. Investigate."

"For *what*?"

"I don't know yet."

Carolina stomped off, and Kick turned for Cash's desk. *Looks just like mine,* she thought, running her hands over the smooth plastic top and along the cool metal underside. *Feels just like mine.*

"I'm not finding anything," Carolina said quietly. "You?"

"Not yet."

"At what point does *your* 'not yet' turn into my *'I engaged in arson because you had a ridiculous idea'*?"

Kick scowled. "About the same time you decided to go along with it?"

Carolina made a disgusted noise and hopped up onto a desktop, trying to get a better look at the vent above a food-pyramid poster.

There has to be something here, Kick thought, checking the window ledge, the pulled-up blinds, the baseboards. *He can't be hearing voices for real.*

She dropped into Cash's desk chair, looked at the whiteboard—and suddenly heard a whisper: "You're a monster."

The hair on the back of Kick's neck stood up. She glanced around. The room was still empty except for Carolina.

"You're a monster," someone hissed.

She faced forward, mouth gone dry. Whoever was whispering and hissing sounded awfully real for someone—or some*thing*—who couldn't exist. "Ca-Carolina?"

"What?"

"Can you come here for a second?" Her voice skidded higher, and she cleared her throat. "Please?"

Carolina huffed, but seconds later joined her. "You're a monster," the voice hissed again, almost verging into a whine. It made Kick's eye twitchy. She glanced at her cousin, and Carolina's eye *also* looked twitchy.

"You hear it too, don't you?" Kick asked.

Slowly, Carolina nodded.

"There's no such thing as curses."

"If there's no such thing, how come you're hearing it too?"

"Because . . . because . . . I haven't figured out that part yet." Kick ran her hands over the desktop again. Still felt the same. She ran her hands under the desktop. Still felt the same. "But it can't be."

"What?"

Kick dropped to the floor and peered up at the desk's metal underside. It looked just like the underside of a desk should look. It was smooth black metal and six crosshatched screws and—

"That's not a screw," she said.

"*What?*"

Kick touched her fingertip to a tiny black disk stuck to the indentation where a screw should have been. It took a little wiggling, but the disk dropped into her palm.

The voice went silent.

She looked from the disk to the chair and back to the disk. "Carolina? Can you sit down in Cash's desk?"

"Not without disinfectant."

"Carolina!"

"Fine!" She sat, kicking Kick in the process.

"You're a monster!" The whiny whisper was immediate. "You're next!"

"That is the *worst*," Carolina hissed, and she was right. Kick could feel the whisper in her teeth and toes.

No wonder he ran for it, she thought. The voice wasn't painful, but it was annoying—deeply annoying. She wiggled out from under the desk and showed Carolina the small disk. "What do you think this is?"

"Irritating." Carolina winced as the voice went off again and covered her ears. "Hold it away from me before it cracks my eardrums."

"You're a monster!" the plastic button cried.

"It didn't go off until one of us sat down." Kick looked at the desk chair. "Can you move?"

"You're a—" Carolina stood, and the voice went

silent. Kick's heart leaped. This felt important. She wasn't sure why.

Yet.

Just like with the desk, she checked the chair. Smooth plastic back. Smooth plastic bottom. Which left . . .

Kick knelt, closely studying the screws at the back of the chair. Sure enough, one wasn't a screw at all. It was another tiny black disk, and this one had a switch on the back. She pried at it with her fingernail, and it popped loose.

"Look." Kick showed the disk to Carolina, who arched one black brow. "Think Mrs. Flagg would know what they are?" she asked.

"Probably, but then she'll want to know where you found them."

Carolina was just *full* of good points. It was annoying.

"Besides," her cousin added, "I know what those are: doorbell sensors. I helped my dad install one at his shop. They don't go off unless there's motion, but I've never heard of one with *voices*. It's usually just a chime."

"Small details," Kick decided. "The important part? The sensors are why it didn't go off until we—or Cash— sat down."

Except Carolina's expression was turning grimmer by the second. Kick didn't understand. This was fabulous. Her brain felt like it was pinwheeling. "*Now* we know why Cash was the only person affected. Plus, being at the back and with the volume turned down, he was the only one who could've heard it."

"But why pick on him? What's he ever done to anybody?"

Yeah. *Why?* "Hold on." Kick ducked under the desk to Cash's right. Another disk. She stood, checked the chair's back. Another disk.

It was the same deal on the desk ahead of Cash's.

And on the desk ahead of that one.

"There are sensors all over the room," Kick whispered, finally turning back to Carolina. "It isn't picking on Cash. It's just *starting* with him. Once all the sensors are activated, you could make the whole class hear that voice. It *proves* there's no—"

Bzzrrriiinnnggg!

It was the first bell, and both girls startled. How had it gotten that late?

Click click click. High heels, and they were headed toward the classroom!

Mrs. Flagg, Kick thought, heart hammering.

"*Mrs. Flagg,*" Carolina whispered, eyes huge.

"I know!"

"Hurry up!"

"I! *Am!*" Kick stuffed the disks into her pocket and hurled herself behind her desk just as the classroom door creaked open.

"You have a decision to make."

Mrs. Flagg swept through the classroom door. "Oh." She stopped, spotting the girls. "Good morning, ladies."

"Good morning!"

"You're next! You're next! You're next!" the disks in Kick's pocket hissed.

Kick winced. Sadly, a layer of canvas coverall did almost nothing to muffle the noise. They were busted. They were *so* busted.

"You're here awfully early." Mrs. Flagg's voice was laced with suspicion.

"Excited to start the day," Carolina said, smiling like she was innocent and perfect and not at *all* like she was lying.

Mrs. Flagg squinted at them. The squint might've meant *Since when?* But it could just have easily meant *I am suspicious, and yet you sound so innocent I am suspicious of my suspicion.* It was a lot to say in a squint, but somehow Mrs. Flagg managed it.

"You're a monster!" the voice squealed. Kick shivered, peeking up at Mrs. Flagg and . . .

Mrs. Flagg's expression hadn't changed a bit. She didn't seem to have noticed. How was that possible?

"Did you see anyone go past?" Mrs. Flagg asked Carolina, tugging at the classroom keys that hung on a lanyard around her neck. "Perhaps someone coming from the school's rear entrance?"

"I didn't think we were supposed to be back there."

"Hmmm. Kick?" Mrs. Flagg's attention switched to Kick. "You didn't happen to leave a Bunsen burner anywhere, did you?"

Kick's mouth went dry. "Oh, no, Mrs. Flagg. That would be dangerous."

Mrs. Flagg's eyes narrowed.

"It's true," Carolina said. "She would never do something like that—besides, she was with me this morning."

"I see." And honestly, Mrs. Flagg really did seem to see everything, but she *still* hadn't acknowledged the whiny voice, so . . .

The classroom door swung open again, and Miss Welty appeared, holding up the remains of the Bunsen burner in her ink-stained fingers. "Nothing?" she asked Mrs. Flagg.

"Nothing," Mrs. Flagg confirmed.

"Monster!" the voice squealed. Kick braced herself. *Surely* they had heard that.

But no.

Miss Welty and Mrs. Flagg chatted about how they hadn't found anything aside from the burner and how no one had seen anything. Miss Welty disappeared down the hallway, taking the Bunsen burner with her, and Kick realized two things: The voice was so annoying her teeth were beginning to itch. And the adults didn't seem to hear it. At all.

Mrs. Flagg turned for her desk, keys jangling. "Class will begin soon. Get your books out."

"Yes, Mrs. Flagg!" But the girls didn't. They watched their teacher instead. They watched her pick up papers. They watched her rearrange pens. They did not watch her wince because the world's most annoying voice was trying to tunnel into her brain through her eardrum.

"You're a monster! You're a monster!"

"How can she *not* hear it?" Carolina whispered when Mrs. Flagg went to the bookshelf to rearrange the Princess Posey titles.

Kick had no idea. Eyes still on Mrs. Flagg, she eased back in her seat and pulled both disks from her pocket. The second one was upside down, revealing the tiny switch on its back. She dug her thumbnail into it and the switch slid down. Silence bloomed.

"Carolina?"

"Yeah?"

"I need to use your internet after school."

Carolina grunted. In agreement? Disagreement? Kick wasn't sure. Then again, she wasn't actually paying attention because she couldn't stop watching Mrs. Flagg's reaction—or rather, her non-reaction.

Kick now knew two things: One, the next several hours were going to be the longest of her life. And two, this now-silent plastic sensor meant the curse wasn't a curse. It meant someone very real was behind it. Someone she could *catch*.

"Why are you grinning?" Carolina asked through gritted teeth.

"It's going to be a good day."

"Kick . . ." her cousin said warningly.

"Carolina," Kick said sweetly. The classroom door swung open, and Natalie May and Mia bounced through.

"Did the spirits tell you about my dad?" Natalie May asked, taking the seat next to Kick. "He's taking me camping this weekend. We decided it last night."

Mia shuddered, sitting down behind them. "I can't believe he's going to risk it. You could run into the Macon twins."

"That's why he's taking us to Boone," Natalie May said, adjusting her sparkly headband. "Do you like camping, Kick?"

"Love it."

Behind her, Carolina made a choking noise, and Kick pretended again not to notice. This was, in fact, a rather huge lie, and after eleven years of knowing each other, Carolina and Kick both knew it. Kick had never understood the appeal of camping. If the outdoors was so wonderful, why were bugs always trying to come inside?

But in Kick's experience, agreeing with someone often made them like you more, and in this case, it *did* seem to make Natalie May relax a little.

And it made something Kick couldn't name tiptoe over her heart. It felt a little like loneliness and a little like guilt, and even though she was sure Natalie May liked her more now, Kick still felt ever so slightly alone.

Which was stupid because she wasn't alone at all. She was surrounded by Natalie May, Mia, and Carolina.

The classroom door swung open again, and the Jennas strutted through. Today, they wore green—green dresses, green headbands, green socks—and their shiny brown hair was loose. It floated around their shoulders like they had their own personal wind machines.

"Good morning!" Mrs. Flagg called, her attention still fixed on the Princess Posey books.

"Good morning!" the Jennas echoed before heading straight for Kick. They strode down the aisle between the desks in unison.

"Well, hello there, *Kick.*" Jenna Jane's smile was

werewolf white. She glanced at Natalie May and Mia and wrinkled her nose. "What are *you* two looking at?"

Mia's ears went pink and Natalie May swallowed, and both girls studied their desktops like they were suddenly fascinating. It made Kick's heart squeeze. She knew what that was like. She knew how that *felt*.

"It's a free country," Kick said. "They can look wherever they want."

"Whatever." Jenna Jane sniffed. "Made your decision yet?"

"I have."

Carolina inched lower in her seat. She was worried, and she shouldn't have been. Kick could feel the plastic buttons' edges pressing into her leg through the pocket of her coveralls.

"And your decision *is*?" Jenna Jane was smiling like she already knew the answer.

Kick took a deep breath, placing one hand on her chest the way Grandma Missouri always did when she was about to confide a deep, dark secret. "I don't usually use my powers for curses, but desperate times call for desperate measures."

"What does *that* mean?" Jenna Jane asked.

Kick curled her other hand around the now-silent plastic button, holding on to it with everything she had. "It means I've decided to lift the curse."

"You must search for the truth."

After all, how hard could it be? No, really. Kick wanted to know. There was no such thing as curses or ghosts or spirits or monsters. Finding the remote sensors proved it!

Or they *would* prove it once Kick figured out why Mrs. Flagg couldn't hear the voice.

And then figured out what to do about it.

"Bottom line," she told Carolina as they walked through the schoolyard after class, "how hard can it be to *pretend* to lift a *pretend* curse?"

"Kick?"

"Yes?"

"Please stop talking." Carolina stomped on, skirt whipping around her knees. The dusty lot was crowded with kids, but they scattered as the cousins came closer. It was kind of like being cursed.

Or maybe they *were* cursed. Girls like the Jennas had their own kind of magic. After Kick had announced she would lift the curse, Jenna Jane had gone a furious shade of red.

Do. Not. Speak to her, she'd said to Jenna B. and Jenna H. Then she'd looked at Carolina. *Or her.*

Which was fine.

Except now the whole class was ignoring them. No one wanted to go against Jenna Jane. Kick understood, but when Natalie May and Mia hurried past her, not looking in Kick's direction even once, she felt like all the air had been kicked out of her.

"Hello?" Carolina elbowed her cousin. Hard. "Are you coming or what?"

"Yeah. Coming."

Uncle Freeport had parked Flubber under the school lane's sole patch of shade. He leaned against the mint-colored car's front fender, watching the grown-ups gathering on the corner to search for the twins. His mouth was stamped into a thin line.

"Dad?" Carolina asked as she opened Flubber's back door. "Can Kick come home with us? We have a group project we're working on."

"Of course." Uncle Freeport said this like it happened all the time.

Or like he's distracted, Kick thought. Her uncle's gaze had switched from the search party to the school. She turned, just in time to see Mayor Burr trotting up the school's front steps.

The mayor only shows up when he wants something, her uncle had said.

What does he want now? What's at the school—?

Carolina hauled Kick into Flubber. "Stop staring!"

"I'm not!" She was. Totally.

Uncle Freeport ambled around to the driver's side and climbed in. He wore his mechanic coveralls again. Today his name tag said *Advice Giver.* "How was school?"

Carolina shoved her backpack onto the floorboards. "It was okay."

"And *you're* okay?" Uncle Freeport watched them in the rearview mirror, and Carolina nodded.

"Yeah."

But you're really *not,* Kick thought. Usually the truth was comforting, but this time . . . not so much.

"Look what was ready for picking," Uncle Freeport said, passing a wrinkled paper bag over the seat.

Carolina opened it, pulling out a red pepper as big as her hand. "Whoa."

"Yep," her father agreed, "looks like our hybrid experiment worked."

Kick perked up. "'Experiment?'"

Carolina dropped the pepper back in the bag. "Dad wanted to show me how cross-pollination works. We crossed a hot pepper with a sweet pepper."

"You can do that?"

Uncle Freeport nodded. "Sure can. As long as the plants are within the same species, it's easy."

"And now we have Hot Flash," Carolina said, tucking the bag down by her backpack.

"'Hot Flash'?" Kick echoed.

"Yeah." Carolina sat up. "That's what we're going to name it."

"But it's not really a flash. I could see you getting a flash when you combine nitrogen monoxide with carbon disulfide—"

"It's a different kind of flash. It's funny," Uncle Freeport added.

It wasn't, but Kick let it go. *All the more reason to get down to business*, she decided as they sped past the turnoff for Uncle Freeport's shop. "Does a doorbell have to ring?"

Carolina stiffened.

"What do you mean?" Uncle Freeport asked.

"Could you record your own message? Like, 'Hey, Freeport, you have visitors!'"

"Why would I want to do that?"

"Because it would be fun?"

Her uncle paused. "Yes," he said at last. "You could. It's not very hard. They use a similar technology in greeting cards—the ones where you record your own message."

"Interesting."

"It is?"

Three minutes later, they made the last turn. It was such a quick walk from school Kick never got why her uncle always picked Carolina up—then she caught him grinning at her in the rearview mirror.

Carolina grinned back. *Oh*, Kick realized. Convenience had nothing to do with it—he picked her up because he liked doing it and this was their thing. Kick's dad had done the same thing when he'd been on sabbatical. She missed that. A lot.

Uncle Freeport steered Flubber to the curb in front of their house. "You girls go on inside. I need to stop by the shop for a few."

Kick perked up. "What a good idea! We could come with you!"

"Not today."

Not any *day*, Kick thought. She'd been asking ever since *forever* to see Uncle Freeport's shop. It had to be amazing. Scientists didn't just give up being scientists, and even though everyone said Uncle Freeport had done just that, Kick didn't believe it. Why else would he be so adamant that she stay away?

There was a conspiracy. Kick was convinced.

"C'mon." Carolina opened the door, and they slid out of the overcool car and into the overwarm sunshine. It had been months and months since Kick had been to her cousin's, but the house looked exactly the same: wedding-cake-white paint, jasmine bushes crowding the porch, and garden gnomes.

Everywhere.

Kick followed Carolina through the front yard's tiny wooden gate and wondered why anyone would want to cover a lawn with short, bearded men. She didn't get to wonder long, though, because the door opened and Aunt Aly appeared.

As always, her glossy brown hair was swept away from her face and twisted into a high knot at the top of her head. As always, her dark blue suit was unwrinkled. Like Mayor Burr, Aunt Aly wore suits everywhere in the Bohring town heat and humidity. Unlike Mayor Burr, she never sweated.

Carolina rushed to meet her. "Hi, Mom!"

"Hi, honey! And Karis!" Aunt Aly clasped one hand to her chest as both girls pounded up the porch steps. "Where's your dad, honey?"

"Shop," Carolina said.

"Huh." Aunt Aly's gaze swept up and down the street, lingering on the shadows that seeped beneath the ancient oak trees. For a heartbeat, she didn't look like Aunt Aly at all. She looked as frightened as the parents from the schoolyard.

"Inside." Aunt Aly waved the girls into the foyer and locked the door behind them.

"Can we use the computer?" Carolina asked.

"For schoolwork?" Aunt Aly's gaze slid over Kick. Worry flickered in her eyes, and Kick knew she was thinking about the kitchen incident.

"It's for extra credit," Carolina said. "It's a . . . guessing game."

"That's fine, but I have a conference call in"—Aunt Aly tapped her phone screen with long fingers—"ten minutes, so please be quiet and don't forget to wash your hands. The both of you. You'll bring home school germs."

In addition to her There's No Such Thing as Supernatural stance, Aunt Aly also believed School Classrooms Are Petri Dishes for Viruses. She was big on antibacterial soap, antibacterial gel, and plastic wrap on all the furniture.

Aunt Aly drifted into the kitchen—or what sometimes served as the kitchen and was mostly Aunt Aly's home office. Carolina turned to Kick. "You know where the bathroom is, right? I'll turn on the computer while you wash up."

Kick pricked to attention. "You mean you . . . aren't?"

Carolina fished around in her pocket. She held up one small bottle of hand sanitizer and then another. "I come prepared."

"Oh." Kick wandered away, down the hallway and toward the bathroom that adjoined Carolina's bedroom. She opened the door, paused, and felt like pieces of her cousin were coming into *much* sharper focus.

This explains so much, she thought, taking in the new glittery pink decor. Before, the bathroom had been fern green. Now it was covered in Princess Posey. There were Princess

Posey towels and Princess Posey pictures and Princess Posey tub faucets. If Kick twisted hard enough, she could probably wrench Posey's head right off—if she wanted to.

Which she suddenly did.

Drying her freshly washed hands on her (not so fresh) coveralls, Kick returned to the living room. Carolina sat at the computer desk, watching the monitor come to life. She slid off the chair and pushed it toward Kick. "Do not look up anything weird. Do not look up anything that could get us in trouble. My mom checks the logs every night, and I'm not getting in trouble because you want to read palms."

"I don't read palms. I have visions."

Carolina's eyes narrowed. She looked a little like Aunt Aly.

And more than a little bit like Grandma Missouri.

"You don't scare me," Kick told her, even though it was kind of scary. She dropped into the chair and Carolina stood behind her. They both stared at the screen.

How to begin? In Kick's opinion, the best results came from asking the right questions—it worked for scientists and psychics—but she didn't know where to start. It wasn't like she could search *uses for remote doorbells*.

Could she?

"Yeah, that's what I thought," Kick grumbled after searching *uses for remote doorbells* and getting thousands of unhelpful results. The air conditioner clicked on, swirling cold and the faint tang of Aunt Aly's perfume around her. Kick chewed her lower lip, fingers hovering over the keyboard.

The right question, she thought. *The right question. The right question.*

Still nothing.

Well, what *did* they know? The remote doorbell sensor was small. You could turn it on and off. It made a noise Mrs. Flagg and Miss Welty couldn't hear, but Kick and Carolina could.

Her breath caught. *That's it!*

What sounds can only kids hear? Kick typed, and skimmed the results. She clicked the first one, and as Carolina leaned over her shoulder, read about high frequencies only kids could hear because their ears hadn't fully matured.

"That's a cool trick," Kick said.

"Unless you're Cash," Carolina added.

"True." She scrolled farther down, and Carolina pressed closer. "So does that explain it? Mrs. Flagg and Miss Welty couldn't hear the voice because it was too high or whatever?"

Kick studied the results. "Must be—and let me take the opportunity to remind you I was right: There's no such thing as curses. Science explains everything."

"Oh, yeah? Does it explain the monsters and the stench?"

"No."

"So . . . what does?"

"I don't know, but I *am* confident we can figure it out," Kick said.

"What is this 'we' stuff?"

"Seriously?"

Carolina gritted her teeth, focusing on the screen. "I still don't understand *why*," she finally said. "*Why* would someone do this?"

Kick shrugged. "They think it's funny?"

"Then why not put crickets in the air vents or superglue the lockers shut?"

"That's happened?"

"No, but it could. I can't be the only person who's thought of that stuff."

"Actually . . ."

Carolina held up one finger as Aunt Aly's voice lifted in the kitchen. She was saying something about calendars and plans, and both girls stiffened.

"Her conference call must be finishing up," Kick whispered.

"Yeah, she's making plans she's going to cancel. I'd say we have ten more minutes. Tops." Carolina paused, gnawing her thumbnail. "Wait. What if they're not doing it to be funny? What if they want everyone scared?"

Kick rolled her eyes so hard they hurt. "Because

they want people to think the curse is coming true?"

"That's exactly what's happening, isn't it?"

"But *why* would anyone want that?"

The girls looked at each other. They looked and looked and—

This is getting nowhere, Kick decided. "Let's think this through." She jumped up and squared her shoulders, channeling Dr. Georgia Winter speaking at a podium. "Who benefits from the curse coming true?" she asked.

"Why do you look like someone just poked you in the back?"

"Just play along," Kick said.

Carolina heaved a huge sigh. "No one benefits."

"Jefferson Burr does. He's selling lucky pennies for a dollar."

"Okay, true. But . . . I don't know. This is pretty drastic. People are *scared.* I wouldn't think Jefferson would take it that far. I mean, think what would happen if his *dad* found out? The mayor wants Bohring to be perfect. Remember how freaked out he was?"

Kick did indeed. The mayor's eyes had skittered around and around in his head while he watched people argue. "Let's say it's not Jefferson, then. Let's assume it's someone else. Who would want people scared?"

"The Jennas. They would think it's funny." Carolina had a gleam in her eye usually reserved for when she got a math problem right. She thought she had the answer, but Kick wasn't so sure.

"Bit high-tech for them, isn't it?"

"Maybe this is a game."

"Kind of stupid to torture themselves, though. The whole class was wired to hear voices. What if it's someone from another grade? What if it's the Macon twins?"

Only, as soon as Kick asked it, she didn't like her line of reasoning. It wasn't . . . reasonable.

In science, if you accidentally dropped a gummy bear into your father's potassium chlorate, you got an impressive smoking effect and a telling-off. If you did it again, you'd get the same results. It was predictable.

But people weren't like that. People were predictably unpredictable. And using a doorbell transmitter to scare someone? That was equal parts weird, organized, and definitely meant they were talking about a person who would be hard to predict.

Predictably unpredictable, Kick thought, frowning.

"You know this doesn't rule out the curse," Carolina said, yanking her back into the moment. "It rules out what happened to Cash, but the Macon twins are still missing, there's still that smell, *and* the monsters. Maybe someone's taking advantage of the moment, but the curse is still playing out like predicted.

"It could still be . . . real."

23

"And once you find the truth, you will have to decide what to do with it."

"Forget what I said earlier," Carolina said. "We have to tell someone. I'll get Mom."

Kick's heart leaped. "Um, let's think about that."

"There's nothing to think about." Carolina jumped to her feet, skirt whispering across the couch's plastic cover. "We have to tell a grown-up about the sensors. That's a mean trick."

She was right and Kick knew she was right, and yet she couldn't shake the memory of Jenna Jane's nasty smile. If they turned in the doorbell sensors, how would she "lift" the curse? How would she win back Natalie May and Mia?

I won't, Kick thought, and ducked in front of her cousin, blocking her from heading into the kitchen. "But how do we explain where we found it? Or *when* we found it?"

Her cousin flinched.

"Exactly," Kick said. "It'll lead them straight to the Bunsen burner and the smoke and *us.*"

Now they both cringed. Out in the kitchen, Aunt Aly ended her work call and clanked some dishes together. Carolina's eyes went from Kick to the door and lingered.

She's going to tell, Kick thought, panic turning her palms sticky. "And what about our Jenna Jane problem? If we turn the sensors in to the grown-ups, the curse won't be lifted and Jenna Jane will make our lives miserable. There *has* to be a better way."

"Like *what*? Letting you have another vision?"

Kick gasped. "Exactly! We'll still turn the sensors in. We'll just be a bit . . . creative with how we do it. To keep up our end of the agreement, we have to make it look like we lifted the curse. Having a vision would do it—especially since the vision will reveal the sensors. It'll prove the whole thing is a legend and someone is taking advantage." Kick paused to think about it. Her mind felt like it was flying, like *she* was flying. The solutions were coming fast and hard. She almost couldn't keep up with them. "I can say I'm having visions of a bad person doing something bad. Pretty sure that's a safe assumption."

"No one is ever going to believe you."

"Yes, they will. It's all in—"

"How you sell it," her cousin finished. "You're not the only one with a fake-psychic grandma, and I *still* don't think Jenna Jane is going to let you go on this one."

"We'll see," Kick said, sounding awfully confident for

someone who maybe, sort of, *kind* of agreed with her cousin.

It was slightly disturbing. Agreeing with Carolina was starting to become a habit.

Time to change tactics, she thought, lifting her chin. "It won't matter if the Jennas don't believe as long as everyone *else* believes. If the curse has taught us anything, it's that."

Carolina still didn't look convinced. She plucked at the end of one of her braids and gave Kick a sideways glance. "How are you going to put the sensors back without getting caught?"

Kick grinned, and it made Carolina's eyes go round. "No way," she said. "We are not going to set something on fire or explode something or do whatever it is you're thinking."

"I was *thinking* about a smaller distraction."

"Like what?"

"I'm still working out the details."

"Which ones?"

All of them. But Kick wasn't about to tell Carolina that. "It'll be a surprise," she told her. *For both of us.*

***

Uncle Freeport took Kick home after dinner. He'd changed out of his mechanic's coveralls but was still wearing his Freeport Garage baseball hat. The brim threw his eyes in shadows, and that seemed to fit his mood. He was the quietest he'd ever been as he drove her home, his hands tightening and loosening, tightening and loosening against the steering wheel.

Is he worried? Kick wondered. Because he seemed worried. This was probably what Grandma Missouri meant when she said, *You can tell everything you need to know by reading a person.* Or maybe Uncle Freeport was doing hand exercises.

"I'll pick you up Monday morning," he said, stopping Flubber at the top of the crooked path. "Your aunt doesn't want you wandering around with all this going on."

"Okay." Kick hopped out, and Uncle Freeport waited until she crossed the crooked bridge before he turned Flubber around. The mint-colored car spun dust into the air, turning the early evening sunshine cloudy.

"Hi, Figgis," Kick called as she passed. The alligator thrashed his tail and ducked under the water.

"Hello to you too, Kick," Kick said, deepening her voice until she sounded suitably alligator-like. The Hollows' Christmas lights twinkled and buzzed as she trotted up the porch steps and let herself inside. Her grandmother's voice drifted down the hallway, and Kick followed it, eventually finding her in the kitchen.

A pot was bubbling on the stove, and something was banging inside it—not that Grandma Missouri noticed. She had the cordless phone wedged between her ear and shoulder. Whoever was on the other end had her spellbound. She startled when she finally noticed Kick.

"Kick!" she said to Kick.

"Here she is!" she said to the caller.

It was Kick's mom. Had to be. She grinned as Grandma Missouri passed her the phone. "Hi! How's work?"

Her mother's laugh barreled down the line. "Amazing! How's Bohring?"

"Not so amazing." Over at the stove, Grandma Missouri checked the bubbling pot and said rude things under her breath. Whatever was in the pot banged harder. Kick dropped into a seat and cradled the phone close. "Did Grandma Missouri tell you about the curse and monsters?"

Her mother made a *humph* sound. "She did. It's utter nonsense."

"Yeah. Everyone's pretty worked up, though. They think the curse is coming true."

She could hear the smile in her mother's voice when she said, "But you don't, of course."

"No."

"That's your scientific mind. I will always be grateful for it."

The compliment made Kick's heart soar high . . . and then plunge. What would her mother think of her pretending to be psychic? The idea slid down her spine to feed.

Grandma Missouri left the pot bubbling and knocking and took a basket of green beans onto the porch.

"Kick?"

"Yeah?"

"Please don't go investigating, okay? Panicked people are dangerous. I don't want you involved."

"Mom—"

The connection went crackly. "Your dad's here! I'm going to put you on speaker, okay?"

Before Kick could answer, her father's voice—warm and deep—filled her ear: "Hey, sweetheart!"

"Hi!"

"I miss you, honey." It threatened to squeeze Kick breathless.

"I miss you too."

Her mother laughed. "I miss you more."

It was an old game, but it still made Kick smile. "Are you keeping up with your experiment notebook?" her father asked. "We can't wait to try out your theories when we get home."

And *that* threatened to squeeze Kick breathless too. "Yeah, I have a bunch of ideas."

"Wonderful!" There was more crackling. For a second, the connection sputtered.

"Is the school very dreadful?" her mother asked.

"No, it's okay." And she was surprised to realize it was. Bohring Elementary and Middle School was quite okay. "Except for the Jennas. They're awful."

"Jennas? In my time, they were the Heathers. There are always girls like the Jennas or the Heathers. Don't let them bother you."

"How?"

"What do you mean?"

"How do you *not* let them bother you? I don't fit in very well already, and then they make sure of it."

There was the longest pause on the other end. "But why would you want to fit in?"

Kick went silent. Her mother went silent. It was the first time they hadn't agreed on everything.

"Honey? Are you there?"

"Yeah. I'm here."

Worry entered her mother's voice: "We'll be home soon. Just force your way through things right now. Once you're out of school, real life begins."

Kick tried to picture it and . . . couldn't. Right now, life without the Jennas seemed so far away as to be impossible. She gripped the phone a little tighter.

Click click click.

"Mom? Mom!"

The line went dead. *It's just a disconnect,* Kick told herself, but the loneliness that she would've sworn wasn't loneliness still threatened to pull her through the floor. She couldn't think past it, and then quite suddenly she could:

I'm going to figure the curse out and be my own super scientist. It should've been a steadying thought, one that centered her and gave her a plan, but now that the pot had stopped bubbling and knocking and her parents' voices were gone, Kick could hear her breath: too fast, too shallow. She jumped down and grabbed her book bag from the floor. She fished out the notebook, flipped past the Monster Hypothesis, and wrote:

Where do feelings go?

She slammed the notebook shut. But the question followed her. Where *did* feelings go? Did they disappear? Or did they leave a residue? Would the ugly twisty feeling in her chest leave a chemical fingerprint on her mind?

She didn't know. Maybe it would rewire her neurons and protons as she sat here.

Maybe it had already.

"Oh, yes. I see everything falling into place for you. Soon too."

Night had finally come to the Hollows. Shadows gathered in the corners of the porch and seeped under Grandma Missouri's rocking chair. Somewhere in the swamp, something even heavier than Figgis splashed, but Kick barely noticed. She banged out the Hollows' back door and slouched into the rocking chair next to her grandmother.

"Did you have a good talk?" Grandma Missouri asked, passing Kick a handful of beans to snap.

"I guess. They had some bad reception. I lost them."

"I'm sorry. The phone systems there need a lot of work— actually, everything does. That's why your parents' work is so important. They'll call again when they can."

"I know." And Kick did. It just hurt. She flicked the bean ends into the water below them. They landed with light *plop-plop*s. Figgis floated into the light to investigate, only his eyes and nostrils showing.

"I miss them too," Grandma Missouri said.

High on the slope that led down to the Hollows, car headlights panned past and then stopped at the gate. Kick flicked away more bean ends. "Readings on a Friday night?"

"May Beth's had a hard time lately. Her boyfriend left her, and she wants to know why."

"Shouldn't she know what happened?"

"I'm sure she knows the events." Grandma Missouri threw more bean ends into the water. It made her bracelets jangle. "It's the *why* that troubles her. Why is the question no one asks, and it's the hardest to answer."

That didn't seem quite right. Kick asked why all the time. She was even asking herself why right now, as in *Why on earth would May Beth care?* Up on the slope, the headlights went dark, and seconds later, the gate creaked open.

Kick watched the dark and felt her grandma watching her. "Why did you stay here?" Kick asked.

"In the Hollows, or in Bohring?"

"Both. Either." She paused. *"Both."*

"Can't seem to pull myself away. Magic is all around this town." It was still too warm, but her grandmother shivered, studying the trees. "It's the swamp that makes it."

Kick tried to see whatever she was seeing. She couldn't. The Bohring swamp didn't look magical. It looked . . . hungry. Trees dug into the water, roots like claws. Silvery moonlight made bone-white faces in the branches, and no matter the time of day, fireflies danced in the distant shadows.

"Far as I can tell," Kick said, "the swamp makes mosquitoes and creepy."

"I didn't say it was pretty magic. I think the swamp makes people around here more themselves—whether that's a good thing or not depends on the person."

Kick thought that over. "Should I go check on May Beth? The path isn't that long. She should be here."

"She'll be here when she comes. If she needs a moment, let's give it to her." The breeze stirred again, making the moonlight wink. "How are you getting on at school?"

"It's fine." Kick picked a green bean stem off the knee of her coveralls. "Jefferson Burr is selling lucky pennies to ward off the curse."

"Huh. We'll see how that turns out for him."

"You're not annoyed? That's horning in on your business."

One corner of her grandmother's mouth twitched. "I think I'll survive. I'm not surprised he's in the thick of it. His father was just the same as a boy."

"You knew the mayor?"

"Of course, did you think grown-ups were always grown-up?"

Kick hadn't thought much about grown-ups at all, but that seemed even worse to admit.

"Burr loved to create trouble," Grandma Missouri

continued, dumping a handful of snapped beans back into their basket and brushing off her hands. "Now he wants everything to be perfect. No trouble. All smiles. His perfect town. I'll bet he's sweating it with the election coming up. His new competition is going to be fierce . . . and unusual."

Her snapping had increased in speed and ferocity. Kick could tell there was more to this, but she didn't know what. She flicked her own bean ends into the water and watched for Figgis.

"You're quiet," her grandmother said. "What are you thinking about?"

"Whether Figgis is trying to eat May Beth."

"You think too much."

Kick felt she didn't think enough. After all, there was the curse to lift and the sensors to replace. She needed to do something about the Macon twins—and what about Cash? Would he ever come back to school?

There was a scuff in the dark, and May Beth—face red and puffy—stepped out of the shadows. She climbed the Hollows' front steps and gave them a wobbly smile. "Evening."

"Evening," Grandma Missouri said, sweeping the last of her beans into their basket. "Can you take this for me?" she asked Kick.

"Sure."

"I hope this is okay." May Beth twisted her handker-chief so hard the veins in her hands stood up like rope. "I just really need some clarity."

"Of course it's okay." Grandma Missouri gave her a rib-cracking hug, her bracelets probably digging halfway through poor May Beth's spleen. "I'm so glad you came."

May Beth sniffed. "I just need to know. I think it will make everything simpler."

"Simpler is definitely better," Grandma Missouri assured her, steering May Beth into the house.

Simpler is never *better*, Kick thought as Figgis resurfaced, whipping his tail from side to side so water rose up in waves. "Simpler is never—"

And *that* was when the solution hit her.

***

It was the longest weekend of Kick's life. Not only did she have to spend most of it ushering customers in and out of the Hollows, but Grandma Missouri had decided to up her game with good-luck charms that involved newt eyes and adder tongues.

Or for civilians: skinned grapes and peeled Twizzlers.

After cutting up precisely 395,902 of them, Kick had called Mia ("She's visiting her cousins," her father had said) and then Natalie May ("She's still out camping," her mother had said), and even though both excuses were understandable, Kick couldn't dismiss the undercurrent of worry swirling through her. By Monday, she was ready to go back to school. Even if it meant confronting the Jennas.

Or revealing the doorbell sensors.

Whichever came first.

She'd kept one of the sensors close (for luck and maybe for reminding her that curses couldn't be real), and it felt like it was burning a hole in her pocket. It wasn't, of course—no, really, she'd checked it twice. Her nerves just made it *feel* like the sensor was burning.

Another question for the experiment book, Kick thought, standing at the top of the crooked path and watching for Flubber. *Can feelings change the, well,* feel *of something?* They certainly seemed to right now.

A dust cloud rolled up the horizon, and Flubber rolled up next, backfiring. "Morning," Uncle Freeport said as Kick opened the back door. Today his name tag said *Believer.*

Carolina scooted over so Kick could climb in next to her. "Hey."

"Hey."

Carolina wore a dress (again), frilly socks (again), and an enormous hair bow (new, but hideous). Kick couldn't stop staring at it.

"Don't," her cousin warned. "Just don't."

"I didn't say anything."

"You said it with your face."

"That isn't even a thing," Kick said, but she looked out the window anyway because it probably *could* be a thing where that hair bow was concerned.

Uncle Freeport swung Flubber around, heading for Bohring, and turned up the radio. The news was on. The announcer was talking about an upcoming cold snap.

"You hear that, girls?" Uncle Freeport tapped two fingers to the dash. "We're going to get a break from the heat."

"And next up, more news," the announcer continued. "Bizarre details are coming in from the small town of Bohring, where people are reporting missing children and mysterious *voices*—"

Uncle Freeport made a choking noise and turned it off. *Like that helps,* Kick thought, glancing at her cousin.

Carolina frowned. "It's okay, Dad. You can listen. We won't get scared."

Uncle Freeport rubbed his forehead like it hurt. "I think everyone's scared right now. Miss Adis told Miss Sonder, who told your mother that Miss Cleo went to Mayor Burr this morning. She told him she'd withdraw her endorsement for his reelection if he didn't do something about Cash and the twins."

"What'd Mayor Burr say?" Kick asked.

"Nothing repeatable." They made the last turn to school, and Uncle Freeport angled Flubber under a patch of shade. "Have a good day!"

"Oh, we will!" Kick grinned. In fact, replacing the sensors and solving the curse would probably make it a great day. She hopped out, Carolina hopped out after her, and Uncle Freeport drove away in a cloud of blue smoke.

"Do you have a plan?" Carolina asked, watching the smoke spiral into the sky.

"Yep. We're gonna reveal the whole thing—all the sensors and how they're on *all* the desks."

"That's *it*?"

"Well, *no*. I'll reveal it with a vision close to the end of school, like a few minutes before class ends. That way everyone will need to head home and we can avoid major questions, but *still* get credit for lifting the curse." She paused, waiting for her cousin to agree, and when she didn't, Kick added, "Simpler is always better, you know."

"Since when have you thought simpler is better?"

"You have another idea?"

Carolina sighed. "No."

"That's what I thought."

"Be subtle. People will pay closer attention if they think you're up to something."

Stand up. Grab your forehead like it's in a vise. Ask "the spirits" what they're trying to say. Then point a finger at the closest desk and reveal the sensors. Simple. Right?

So why was Kick's stomach so knotted?

The classroom clock inched toward 8:30 a.m. Homeroom hadn't even started, and Kick felt like she was going to be sick.

Gonna be a long day, she thought, trying to glance casually around the classroom. Her eyes skimmed all the corners, all the students, and fell on Natalie May—who looked down and didn't look back up.

On the other side of the room, Jenna Jane laughed. Not because she'd noticed Natalie May ignoring Kick—although that probably *would* have made her laugh—but because she was whispering with the other Jennas. She belonged in Bohring, and for three whole heartbeats, Kick knew she didn't. She liked science, she enjoyed a good explosion, and she was dangerously close to being outed as a fake psychic. Having friends in Bohring was never going to work. She'd been kidding herself.

Then came the knock at the door.

"Good morning," Dr. Callahan said to Mrs. Flagg, stepping inside. Her heels were high, her suit was impeccable, and her blond hair was slicked back into a tight bun. Kick still wanted to know how she did that. Superglue? It seemed entirely possible.

"Is everything okay, Malinda?" Mrs. Flagg asked.

"I'm ready to speak with your class now."

"Oh." Their teacher touched one hand to her mouth. It did not, Kick noticed, have glitter on it today, but there were dark shadows underneath her eyes. It looked like Mrs. Flagg had joined the search for the twins over the weekend.

Bzzrrriiinnnggg!

Mrs. Flagg faced the class. "This is Dr. Callahan, our school counselor—"

"Psychologist," Dr. Callahan corrected.

"*Psychologist*, and she's here to speak with you about the, ah, incident."

"Which one?" Jenna Jane asked.

"Cash's incident," Mrs. Flagg said.

That's what we're calling it? Kick glanced at Carolina and saw the same skepticism.

Dr. Callahan smiled like she was in a toothpaste ad and brushed off her sleeve. Tiny bits of hair floated into the air. "What happened to Cash was a terrible thing. A very terrible thing. Does anyone have any questions about it? Because you can talk to me about anything. Even your worries—*especially* your worries. That's what I'm here for. Talking. Confiding. Helping—"

The classroom door swung open, and Jefferson Burr hustled through, shoelaces flapping and pockets jingling.

Lucky pennies are still a booming business, Kick thought.

"No questions?" Dr. Callahan's voice scraped upward, desperation edging in as Jefferson dropped into his desk. "Maybe something's going on that you don't understand?"

Or maybe something that you *don't understand,* Kick thought. It didn't seem like Dr. Callahan had a clue what was going on. She was fishing the students for answers. That was . . . kind of scary.

"Is anyone worried about what happened to the Macon boys?" Dr. Callahan asked. "Anyone at all?"

More silence.

"Well," she said, drawing her shoulders back, "since no one seems upset, I'll take my leave. Isadora? A moment, please."

Mrs. Flagg seemed to grimace as she followed

Dr. Callahan to the door. The two exchanged whispers before the door clicked shut and Mrs. Flagg faced the class once more. "Open your science books to page twenty."

Kick bent to get her book—and a sudden thought crept across her mind: *Whoever stuck the sensors under the desks had access to the classroom.*

The *locked* classroom.

A kid wouldn't have a key, she realized, palms going clammy. Which meant the prankster couldn't be the Macon twins or Jefferson *or* the Jennas.

It had to be a grown-up.

"You didn't see this coming? Well, I did."

In Kick's experience, discoveries were happy things. Even if something exploded, you knew, at a minimum, not to do whatever caused the explosion again. It made things simple. This discovery, though? This one wasn't happy, and it certainly wasn't simple.

It was *scary*.

So, in the spirit of sharing, Kick told Carolina.

"A grown-up?" her cousin repeated as they waited for lunch. The air was thick and damp and warm. The line inched forward. The girls inched with it.

Kick tried for a practical tone: "At least, it narrows our suspects, right?"

"It does not." Carolina leaned close. "Look around."

Kick did. Bohring Elementary and Middle School might have been the smallest school she'd ever attended, but there were still plenty of people to pick from—Miss Welty,

Mrs. Flagg, Miss O'Connor, Principal Locke. Lots of adults with access to Mrs. Flagg's classroom.

"And what if someone *stole* the classroom key?" Carolina added. "That could happen."

The line moved up again. They took red lunch trays from the stack. Kick craned her head, trying to see the food options: beef Stroganoff or beef with noodles. *Such choices,* she thought.

"But how would someone steal a key?" she whispered. "Mrs. Flagg wears her school keys around her neck, on that lanyard thing. Maybe she got knocked out?" She paused, considering this. "No, that won't work. Someone would have to have access to chloroform."

"Or a really big stick."

"True." Kick watched Mia and Natalie May sit down at a nearby table. She waved, but couldn't catch their attention. "But this is a town of four hundred and fifty-three people. We would've heard about a traumatic brain injury. It *has* to be an adult with classroom access—plus, what kid would buy doorbell sensors?"

Carolina shrugged. "None."

"Exactly." Kick took a deep breath, ready to impart wisdom to her cousin—wisdom she'd learned from reading a single murder mystery the summer before, but still wisdom. "Our theories have to match the facts. We can't twist the facts to match our theories."

Carolina set her tray down and gave Kick a hard look. "Oh, yeah? So why would a grown-up do this? You have a fact for that?"

"I do not," Kick told her, mustering as much dignity as possible. "But I will."

"This really isn't good."

"No. It's not."

"We need to stay out of it."

"We *will*. As soon as we get Jenna Jane to back off." Kick caught Mia and Natalie May watching them, but as soon as Kick waved, they looked away. "Ten minutes before the bell. Be ready."

"I—"

Kick carried her tray to Natalie May and Mia's table and smiled at them like her hands weren't shaking. "Can I—" Kick felt Carolina behind her. "Can *we* sit with you?"

It was a bold move. Everyone knew the Jennas weren't speaking to them, and Kick could *see* Natalie May and Mia remember that when they looked at each other.

Please, she thought, *I would do it for you.*

"Okay," Natalie May said at last.

"Can I sit too?" Carolina's eyes stayed on her tray.

"Of course you can." Kick scooted over to make room, and her cousin sat down. "How's practice for the play going?" she asked Mia. "Do you need any help?"

Mia paused. "No, I'm good."

"That's great!" And it was, wasn't it? Kick focused on her beef Stroganoff. Or was it beef with noodles? She suddenly couldn't remember which she'd picked because all she could feel was her friends' friendliness draining away. Like Natalie May and Mia were disappearing right in front of her.

What did I do? she wanted to ask, but she knew the answer. She'd annoyed the Jennas. She'd been herself. She'd . . .

She'd have to fix this.

***

Hours later, the clock above Mrs. Flagg's whiteboard inched toward 3:15 p.m. Kick was pretending to concentrate on a math problem, and Carolina was pretending to have a coughing fit.

At least Kick was pretty sure she was pretending.

When her cousin had first coughed, Kick had looked toward her with concern.

"No," Carolina had mouthed.

"Yes." Then Kick had faced the whiteboard.

Now it was ten minutes later, and Carolina was still at it.

COUGH! COUGH! COUGH!

"Carolina, do you need to go get some water?" Mrs. Flagg asked.

To Carolina's credit, she really did sound like she

needed some. "No," she said weakly. "I'll be fine." But she stared at Kick like she wanted to set her on fire.

Kick stared right back and then . . .

The clock ticked to 3:15 p.m.

Go big or go home, she thought, and leaped to her feet. "A vision!"

Everyone turned. Kick moaned, pressing the back of her hand to her forehead. "I see . . . sound . . . sound radiating out like waves of light."

"Oh, *please,*" Jenna Jane said. "Not this again."

"She's having a vision!" Carolina yelled, and then slapped one hand across her mouth like she couldn't believe she had yelled.

Kick couldn't believe it either.

"That's enough, you two," Mrs. Flagg said. "Kick? Please sit down."

Kick pointed a shaky finger toward the back of the classroom. "Whatever drove Cash to hurl himself from our presence . . . it's on everyone's desk!"

"What on earth are you talking about?" Mrs. Flagg asked.

"Look." Kick lifted her shaky finger a bit higher, wondered if it was too much, and decided it wasn't. "Look for yourself. The spirits say we must."

"That's . . . ridiculous," Mrs. Flagg managed, but she

must've been spooked too—or at least curious—because her gaze drifted to the closest desk.

And stuck.

Everyone in the class went silent.

Mrs. Flagg put down her whiteboard marker. "Kick, if this is some sort of joke, it's in very poor taste and it's extremely disruptive." She looked down at Henry Omoto, sitting frozen in his chair. "Henry, please stand up."

He leaped up and Mrs. Flagg ran her hands along his chair, over his desktop, and then under it. Her expression showed nothing and nothing and . . .

There! Mrs. Flagg's eyes flew wide, and she pulled out the sensor, holding it in her open palm.

Kick tried to look baffled. It didn't work, so she tried for humble. Also didn't work. "The spirits really know what they're talking about, huh?"

Mrs. Flagg leveled her a flat gaze. "Principal's office. *Now.*"

"Things are never so bad that they can't get worse."

Mrs. Flagg said nothing as she walked Kick down to Principal Locke's office. Since the school was so small, it wasn't a long walk, but it was plenty of time for Kick to think about her plan's biggest flaw: By pointing out the sensors, she'd implicated herself.

Rookie mistake, Kick thought, frowning. *Or maybe it's a Learning Moment. That sounds better even if the end result is the same.*

Mrs. Flagg knocked on the principal's heavy wooden door.

"Come in," a voice called.

Mrs. Flagg pushed open the door, revealing an office filled with beige carpeting, beige chairs, and beige walls. Even Principal Locke looked a little beige as she sat behind her desk, button-up shirt buttoned to her neck.

"Yes?" she asked, peering at them from over the top of her reading glasses. "Is everything okay?"

"Not quite." Mrs. Flagg stepped forward, steering Kick into one of the armchairs while passing Principal Locke the doorbell sensors. "I just found that under one of the desks in my classroom."

"Oh." The principal's glasses slipped a bit as she peered down at it. "What is it?"

"A doorbell sensor."

Principal Locke nodded, looking up with an expression Kick could only describe as *Is that supposed to mean something to me?*

"They can be programmed for messages," Mrs. Flagg continued. "Cash Hunnicut heard voices before he ran out. *Incessant* voices. I think someone used a doorbell sensor to torment him and whoever it was also intended to use them to torment the rest of the class."

Principal Locke's eyes widened. She sat back in her chair, making it creak. "And why is Miss Winter involved?"

"She found them. During a *vision*."

Principal Locke cocked her head, lips parted. She didn't seem to know where to begin.

Neither did Kick.

Principal Locke studied her. "Did you put the sensors on Cash's desk, Miss Winter?"

"No." It came out smaller than Kick intended. "I didn't do it."

"Then how did you know it was there?"

"Psychic vision. You know how these things go."

Principal Locke frowned like she most assuredly did not. She picked up the receiver on her phone and dialed a few numbers. "Dr. Callahan? Could you come in here for a moment?"

Seconds later, Dr. Callahan glided into the office, pointy shoes silent on the beige carpet. "Thank you for joining us," Principal Locke said, and then outlined everything that had happened.

Dr. Callahan stared at Kick. "This is a very serious offense," she said at last. "You need to tell us the truth: Did you do this?"

Kick swallowed. "No."

The adults looked at each other. They didn't believe her. She swallowed again. "When would I have done it?"

"You were in my class early yesterday," Mrs. Flagg said.

"Yes, but that was after Cash ran."

Everyone thought about this. The adults seemed to relax a tiny bit. "So who *did* put them there?" Mrs. Flagg asked.

"Someone awful. Obviously," Kick added.

Dr. Callahan's mouth went thin. "There's no way this was a vision. You saw someone put the sensors under the desks."

Stick to your story, Kick told herself, and forced a shrug. "I can't explain the mystical forces."

Dr. Callahan's eyes bugged. "Try."

"I can't. Your aura is still too . . . green."

Dr. Callahan's eyes bugged even more.

"I don't know what that means," Principal Locke said, "and I don't want to know. What about the Bunsen burner incident? Do you know anything about that?"

"Bunsen burner?" Kick tried to channel Innocent Carolina. *"What* Bunsen burner incident?"

Bzzrrrriiinnnggg! As she stood there in Principal Locke's office, the bell sounded far away. School was over, but no one moved.

"Is she capable of such things?" Principal Locke asked as student shouts and laughs swelled in the hallway. "I've never heard of Karis or Carolina ever being suspected of bullying. Plus, she would have to know how to do . . . this." Principal Locke turned one sensor over and over, and finally, settled it upside down.

"She's certainly smart enough to figure something like that out," Mrs. Flagg said.

It didn't feel like a compliment.

"Maybe it's a cry for attention," Dr. Callahan said. She sat down in the chair next to Kick and scooted it closer. Too close. Kick could see the beginnings of more sunburn on the psychologist's neck and some sort of fur on her pants.

"After all, the child does have an interesting family life. Perhaps she's imitating what she sees at home."

All three adults seemed to consider this, and in the silence, Kick could hear the *tick tick tick* of the clock.

"Or maybe it's real," Mrs. Flagg said, playing with the keys slung around her neck. "My sister sees Miss Missouri every other Thursday, and she says her predictions are very accurate. What if it's hereditary?"

Dr. Callahan snorted. But Principal Locke nodded. "My great-uncle Jessup goes as well. Says he can't make a decision about the farm without consulting her."

The adults turned back to Kick.

"I want to be fair here," Principal Locke said. "We can't prove you planted the transmitter, so you won't be punished, but, Miss Winter?"

"Yes?"

Principal Locke leaned forward. "We'll be watching you."

28

"No good deed ever goes unpunished."

Mrs. Flagg's classroom was empty when Kick skidded in, panting from her sprint. She scrambled around, gathering up her things, and bolted. Just like before, her sneakers sounded far too loud, clattering against the floor, but Kick didn't care. She ran through the school's double doors and leaped off the steps, legs churning.

And a shadow slid out from her left.

"Kick!" Carolina rushed toward her. "I was so scared!"

"Me too." Kick slumped against the spiny, spiky fence. "They think I'm behind the doorbell sensors or that I know who is."

Carolina made a choking noise.

"I know, right? Principal Locke says I'm not in trouble—they can't prove I had anything to do with it—but she *also* says they'll be watching me." Kick took a moment to arrange and then rearrange the books in her backpack.

It didn't help. Her hands were still shaking. "It's worth it, right? We revealed the plan. Principal Locke knows something's going on."

Carolina nodded. "Yeah, that's the important part."

Just outside the gates, Jefferson Burr climbed into the mayor's black limousine and slammed the door. Blue smoke screeched from under the tires as the limo carried him away.

"I wonder if any of them will ever know we saved them," Carolina said, watching the smoke curl into nothing. "Being a hero isn't nearly as glamorous as I thought it would be."

"You've thought about being a hero?"

She shrugged. "Yeah. Thought my outfit would be better, though."

They both looked down at Carolina's frilly dress and equally frilly ankle socks. They were especially white next to Kick's dirty sneakers.

"Will you be in trouble for waiting on me?" she asked. "You're going to be late."

Her cousin shrugged. "It'll be okay. Mom is probably headed this way already. I'll meet her on the road. She'll be happy once she sees I'm not dead in a ditch."

"She worries about that?"

"She worries about everything."

They scuffed through the yellowed grass, heading for

the gate. Without the other kids, the schoolyard felt hushed, as if it were holding its breath. Kick hated it. "Well," she said, "at least the worst is over."

"How's that? There's still the smell and the glow and the missing Macon boys—"

"I meant it can't get any worse for *us*."

"Oh, yeah?" Carolina smirked. "Wait until Principal Locke calls Grandma Missouri."

***

Carolina is so annoying, Kick thought, trudging across the Hollows' crooked bridge. Up on the porch, Grandma Missouri waited for her, arms crossed and expression crosser.

"Karis. Winter."

Remember, she told herself, *you had almost nothing to do with any of it.*

Which should have been more comforting.

"Hi," Kick called, smiling the smile of someone who had nothing to hide.

Her grandmother glowered.

"I am so dead," Kick muttered to Figgis as she passed over his head. Figgis dipped under the inky water, which Kick assumed was the way alligators said, *I agree.*

And probably, *I disagree.*

And even more probably, *Go get my chicken cutlets.*

Kick trudged up the porch steps, and Grandma

Missouri pointed her cane toward the ceiling. "*What* were you thinking?"

At the moment? Kick was thinking that Grandma Missouri loved to ask that question. "About what?"

"About all of it. You're having visions now?"

She grimaced. "Yeah . . . it seemed like a good idea at the time."

"Well, that's true enough for a lot of things, but you're going to have to explain far more than that." Grandma Missouri opened the door, limping slowly back inside. The hallway and living room were dim, their lamps covered with silk scarves Grandma Missouri had found at yard sales—but the kitchen was bright as ever. The yellow paint glowed, and fat-bodied flies hurled themselves against the windows, desperate to get at the overhead lights inside. The taxidermied squirrels, Larry and Gary, still lay on the table, half-dressed.

"Now," Grandma Missouri said, bracing her back against the countertop edge, "tell me the truth. What's going on?"

"I told people at school I was . . . psychic. It kind of back-fired, and the meanest girl in Bohring challenged me to lift the curse."

Grandma Missouri blinked then blinked again. "You know, I almost miss the days when you used to run around with your fingers in your ears."

Kick scowled. "I didn't run around with my fingers in

my ears. I was *covering* my ears because I was testing sound waves."

"With yarn from my knitting and coat hangers from my closet."

"Well . . . yeah. The sound travels up the yarn and—"

"Why would you tell people you're psychic?"

Kick's throat stuck. "They didn't like who I was, so I made up someone else. I wanted things to be different this time."

"Mission accomplished." Her grandmother paused. "And?"

"And I'm not sure they're going to leave me alone. Jenna Jane seemed pretty unimpressed with my vision."

Grandma Missouri's fingers began to drum on the countertop. "I meant, *and* how did you plan all this? *And* how did you know about the doorbell sensors? *And* how did you even know to look under the desks for them?"

"Oh." Kick straightened. "Well, technically speaking, that was a bit of a happy accident. We knew something was going on because the curse always works in a pattern: smell, hear, see, right? Well, Cash was hearing stuff well before the smells, so we knew it had to be an aberration, and *then* we found the sensors, and *then* we figured out what we were going to do about it."

"'We'?"

"Carolina and me."

Her grandmother's fingers slowed their tapping.

"Together, huh? I'm assuming revealing those sensor things with a vision was your idea?"

Kick nodded.

"Of course, it was." Grandma Missouri rubbed one hand across her face. "Okay, I'll give it to you: That was smart, but the next time you feel a 'vision' coming on, remember to put your fingers to your temples. Don't put your hands in the air like you're some faith healer. We have a reputation to remember."

Kick stopped dead. "I'm sorry . . . what?"

"Don't 'what' me. If someone asks you a middling hard question, put one hand to your temple. If it's a really hard question, put both hands to your temples. You could always try quivering a little bit—like the spirits are shaking you apart—or you could try making your nose look like it's bleeding. You'll need some red food coloring and golden syrup but—" Grandma Missouri frowned. "Never mind. Stick with the one-hand-versus-two-hands tactic. It gets them every time."

Kick smiled. "I don't think I understand."

"Oh, I think you do. I don't approve of this whole pretending to be someone you're not to win friends, but if you're going to do it, do it right. Now go take a bath, brush your teeth, and go to bed. Do you understand *that*?"

"Yes."

Grandma Missouri eyed her. "Also, no more investigating. It's dangerous."

Kick started to agree, but then stopped. Something nameless shuddered through her, a shadow—enormous as an owl's wing—flitted across her back. She couldn't let it go. "But we *should* get involved! We need to find out what's going on! It's always better to know the truth, and we *know* there's no such thing as ghosts or spirits or curses. We *know* that. We lie about them all the time."

"Is that what you think I do?" Grandma Missouri lifted her chin like Kick had taken a swipe at it. "You think all I do is lie to people?"

Um, she thought, *I mean, I could lie and say no, but that would be lying about lying and . . .*

And Grandma Missouri was waiting for an answer.

"Yes?"

Her grandmother leaned down so they were at eye level with each other. "I tell people what they need to hear, and if those people need to believe it's coming from the beyond so they can screw together their courage and do what needs to be done, then isn't that more than just a lie?"

Kick shrugged. She wasn't so sure now. "Why can't you just be *you* and tell them what they need to know?"

"They wouldn't believe me. Sometimes you need to believe the advice is coming from someone who loves you, not from a stranger."

"But—"

"You'll understand when you're older. Go to bed."

"Ah, yes, it's all becoming clear."

Morning came bright and hot and humid—pretty much exactly like every morning in the Hollows, but this time it felt different.

Probably because I'm practically a detective now, Kick thought, pushing her cereal around in circles with her spoon. *The curse of Bohring is completely solved.*

Well, almost entirely completely solved. Yeah, she might have fumbled the reveal, but did Edison stop at his first attempt to develop the lightbulb?

No way, Kick thought, stabbing her spoon into her soggy cereal. *He kept going for another 999 times.*

"That breakfast isn't going to finish itself," her grand-mother said from behind the newspaper. She was reading an article about a trailer park that had been blown away in a tornado, which didn't seem much like news to Kick because, around Bohring, divorce and tornadoes were the fastest way to lose trailers.

Maybe there's an inherent magnetism, Kick thought, staring at the picture of an empty concrete slab. *One for the experiment notebook?*

She eyed her backpack sitting by the door and decided it was too much effort to go get it.

Grandma Missouri turned a page. "You seem sleepy."

"I was up late thinking about the consequences of my actions."

The newspaper twitched down, and Grandma Missouri glared at her. *Do not look away,* Kick told herself. *Do not blink. Do not breathe.*

After a moment, her grandmother flicked the newspaper back up. "I think I hear your uncle pulling up."

Kick doubted her grandmother heard a thing, but she wasn't about to argue. She dumped her cereal in the sink, grabbed her book bag, and dashed out the door, narrowly missing Butler. He hissed and swiped one paw at her ankles.

"Sorry, Butler!" As Kick ran across the crooked bridge, Figgis thrashed and ducked under the water.

Or tried to duck under the water.

Most of his back and sides stayed well above the surface. It might be time to cut back on the chicken cutlets. "Bye, Figgis!"

Kick pounded up the dusty path, hitting the road just as Flubber appeared in a cloud of smoke. Uncle Freeport parked and got out of the car. Today, his name tag said *Likes Dogs.*

"Is everything okay?" Kick asked.

"Couldn't be better. I'll only be a minute." He walked past Kick and down toward the Hollows.

"What's going on with your dad?" Kick asked Carolina as she opened the back door.

"I don't know. He's been at the greenhouse a lot."

Kick paused, her brain roaring much like Figgis roared before a feeding. "Did you say . . . 'greenhouse'?"

"Nope."

"You did."

"I didn't." But Carolina said it in a weird, high-pitched voice that said she absolutely had said "greenhouse."

Kick eyed her, and Carolina arched one brow. She wore that fluffy pink skirt again, the one with ruffles. Knowing what Kick knew now about Aunt Aly's obsession with dressing Carolina, she was pretty sure Aunt Aly had been going for a princess look.

But even Princess Posey would've looked at that skirt and gone, *Nah, too frilly.*

"You grounded?" Carolina asked.

"No. She knows I'm not behind Cash, but she's suspicious I'm up to something else."

Her cousin nodded. "My mom's always suspicious I'm up to something."

"How is that even possible? You're the best-behaved kid I know."

"She thinks you're only as good as the company you keep."

"I can't really fault her on that one."

Uncle Freeport ambled back up the crooked path and climbed into Flubber. "Ready for school?"

Neither girl answered, but Uncle Freeport didn't seem to notice. He put Flubber into drive, stomped on the gas, and away they went.

***

As nice as it was to be driven to school, it also meant Kick couldn't tell Carolina about the night before until they'd reached the schoolyard. As usual, it was hot and crowded. As usual, the Jennas sat in the shade, watching everyone and whispering.

Unlike usual, Jefferson Burr sat by himself.

Lucky penny business must be slow. Kick couldn't stuff down her smile. Then she passed Sheriff Day and Deputy Patel, and that smile evaporated. Sheriff Day was sipping a giant energy drink and watching the trees beyond the spiny, spiky fence, and Deputy Patel was sipping a giant coffee and watching the students inside the spiny, spiky fence. Their bodies were strung tight like they expected something to happen at any second.

"What are they doing here?" she whispered to Carolina.

"Protection. We might've figured out the voices, but the twins are still missing. Mom told Dad that Miss Ruth told Sheriff Day that he better watch that none of the other kids disappear."

"Whoa."

"Yep, and she did it at the diner so everybody heard her. Mom said that was tactical because the mayor isn't the only one up for reelection. She thinks Sheriff Day and Mayor Burr are panicking."

"Oh, look," Jenna Jane said as they walked by. "It's a loser and her side*kick*."

"Who revealed the curse is a big, fat hoax," Kick said. "You're welcome, by the way."

Jenna Jane scowled. "You didn't reveal all of it."

Which was true and annoying, and Kick opened her mouth to say something—anything—but Carolina hauled her away. "C'mon. I have to get my summer camp application signed by Principal Locke."

"What kind of summer camp requires an application *almost a year before*?" Kick asked as they pounded up the school's front steps.

"The kind my mother prefers."

They pushed through the doors. Carolina turned for Principal Locke's office, and Kick turned for Mrs. Flagg's class. She squeezed between some fourth-graders and spotted Natalie May and Mia just ahead. Their bodies turned toward each other like matching question marks, and Kick's heart swung high.

"Hey!" Kick raced up to them. Mia looked at the floor, and Natalie May looked at the air by Kick's right ear. "Is everything okay?"

"Yeah . . . well . . . no," Natalie May said, gaze still pinned to something beyond Kick. "I don't think we should be friends anymore. It's not a good idea."

"I don't either," Mia added, not lifting her eyes.

Kick's whole face went hot. *When I'm a famous scientist,* she thought, *I'm going to discover the secret to disappearing.*

But she really wished she knew the secret now. "Is this because of yesterday?" she managed at last.

"It's because of you. You're . . ." Natalie May trailed off. She looked at Mia, and Mia shrugged.

"You're difficult to be friends with," Mia supplied.

"No—no, I mean . . . not quite." Natalie May looked pained. "You're very nice, but it *is* difficult to be friends with you. It's just that . . ."

It's just Jenna Jane, Kick thought. Some things were more powerful than the truth or a curse.

"Look," she said, hating the desperation edging into her voice, "I know it's been weird, but things are going to get better. The curse is fake. Jenna Jane can't bother us anymore. She can't—"

"Don't, okay? Please?" Mia said.

Kick watched them walk away, heading for Mrs. Flagg's classroom, and felt something inside her rip loose. It trailed after them, and she was glad to see it go. Whatever it was, she didn't need it.

"The curse of Bohring is alive and well."

This is what happens when experiments don't go according to procedure, Kick thought, dragging into Mrs. Flagg's class just as the bell rang. She'd tried so hard. It *should've* worked. She should still be friends with Natalie May and Mia.

But she wasn't.

The Jennas ran in behind her, one of them stomping on the back of Kick's sneaker as hard as she could. Kick winced and slid into her seat, staring straight ahead until Carolina slid in next to her.

"Hey." Her cousin tucked her book bag under her chair like she did this every day. Which of course she didn't, and usually Kick would've pointed this out, but it felt nice to have Carolina next to her.

Maybe even a little more than nice.

Homeroom passed quickly as Mrs. Flagg got down to business. "For the next hour, we're going to work *quietly* on our history projects. Considering the, um, distractions we've had this year, if you'd like to pick a partner to help you, now is the time to do so. Remember, topics must be related to Bohring. And if you have any questions, I'll be available to answer them."

"No questions here," Jefferson said, slipping through the door.

"Jefferson," Mrs. Flagg said, "this is the second time you've been late this week, do you know what that means?"

"That it's Tuesday?" Jefferson sat in his seat, unsold pennies jangling in his pockets. Mrs. Flagg pressed the tip of her index finger to the corner of her eye. It didn't help. Even from here, Kick could see the skin jumping.

"Detention, Jefferson."

"But—"

"I said detention! Everyone, get started on your projects!"

Kick leaned down to take her history book out of her backpack, and Carolina nudged her shoe into Kick's. "There was another monster sighting last night. Dr. Callahan was telling Principal Locke when I came in."

Chills rippled across Kick's skin. "Who saw?"

"Miss Cleo."

"*Who?*"

"She owns the Curl Up and Dye hair salon."

"Oh. Right. She saw them before, didn't she? Maybe she's being targeted?"

Carolina looked over her history book as if it were fascinating. "Or maybe it's a small town, so of course she'd see the monsters again. You know what this means? The curse is still going."

"No way. Whatever's going on can be explained."

"*How?*"

"Always an excellent question," Mrs. Flagg said. Carolina and Kick froze. "I enjoy how you two are always asking how and why and why not." Her hand strayed to the classroom keys around her neck, and she smiled at the girls. "Are you two working together on your project?"

"Absolutely," Carolina assured her.

"Wonderful! And what *is* your topic?"

"How Bohring looks backward to go forward."

What? Kick stared at her cousin, wondering if her headband was too tight.

"It's unusual for such a small town to have such a big interest in its history," Carolina continued. "After all, we don't have a full-time fire department, but we *do* have a historical society. Lots of interest in history around here."

"Oh, how fascinating!" Mrs. Flagg's face lit up. "You'll need to refine your premise a bit more, though. Let me know if you want help."

"Absolutely." The smile was still pure Carolina, and it *stayed* pure Carolina until Mrs. Flagg drifted off to help another student. Then it disappeared. "I hope that's okay," she whispered, smoothing the already-smooth corners of her history book. "I know you probably wanted to work with Natalie May and Mia."

"I don't. It's a long story," Kick added when Carolina started to open her mouth. "And *why* are we looking at the history of Bohring?

Her cousin shrugged. "You're the one who pointed out Cash was an aberration. What if he isn't? What if the rhyme got the procedure wrong?"

"Like someone took artistic license and decided the rhyme sounded better with 'hearing' coming later?"

Another shrug. "It's possible our original data is off. We need to go to the source."

Our? *We*? Carolina might not have noticed those two little words, but Kick certainly did.

"Either way," her cousin finished, "we won't know until we double-check, right?"

"Right."

The girls studied each other.

"No, no, no," Mrs. Flagg said, making her way back to the front of the room. She pulled the white projection screen down from its metal spool and quickly tapped out something on her computer, readying a slide to play. "Look at the map, Jenna Jane," she continued, striding to the class-room door and reaching for the light switch. "The history of Bohring's waterways and fishing industry is fascinating—"

Since when? Kick wondered.

Mrs. Flagg flipped off the light and plunged the classroom into dark.

And the green glowing message scrawled across the projector screen emerged:

THE CURSE OF BOHRING IS HERE. NO ONE WILL ESCAPE.

The Jennas screamed. Mrs. Flagg screamed.

Kick might have screamed a little too. She definitely reached for Carolina's hand—or maybe Carolina reached for hers. Either way, they grabbed each other and held on as the rest of the students jumped to their feet or cowered in their desks.

"It's still happening!" Jefferson yelled, pointing one finger at the message. "We're all doomed!"

More screams went up. Someone started crying.

"It's another hoax!" Mrs. Flagg hurled herself back to the light switch. The room went bright once more, and the words disappeared.

Kick leaned closer to Carolina. "What part of the curse has glowing messages?"

"Dunno."

"It's a hoax," Mrs. Flagg repeated, herding Jefferson back into his seat. "It's a terrible *joke*. Everyone sit down—Jenna

Jane, I mean it. Sit. I need to call Principal Locke. When we find out who did this, he or she will be very sorry."

Kick nudged Carolina. "I think we rattled someone when we found the sensors. What if they're getting panicked? The handwriting's a bit sloppy. Might I even say *shaky* from fear of being discovered?"

"Stop smiling like that. You *might* be onto something, but the Macon boys are still missing."

Kick's smile drained. This was true. "Well, I can't explain that yet, but we're getting there. I can feel it."

"Is it a fuzzy feeling? Like you have ginger ale on the brain? Because that means you're about to pass out. You should go lie down." But Carolina was fighting her own smile. If this had been three weeks ago—heck, even three days ago—there wouldn't have been any smile to fight.

"You know you want to find the answers as much as I do," Kick said, and when Carolina actually *grinned*, she knew she was right.

"You're about to make an unpleasant discovery."

Of course, getting to the historical society was easier said than done. Uncle Freeport seemed less than thrilled when the girls piled into Flubber that afternoon and asked if they could go.

"It's for school research?" he asked, guiding the stuttering, backfiring mint-colored car into the school lane.

"Our history project," Carolina said, once again looking perfectly innocent.

How does she do that? Kick wondered. Maybe the frills helped. It was kind of hard to believe someone was capable of plotting to undermine a fake curse when their lace-trimmed socks matched their lace-trimmed headband.

"Does it need to be today?" he asked, lifting one hand to wave to Mr. Grimp as they passed the convenience store. "I need to do some work at the shop and your mother has back-to-back conference calls."

"We could always walk," Kick suggested, trying for the same innocent tone her cousin had used.

Uncle Freeport's eyes flicked to the rearview mirror. "I'll drop you off and come back to pick you up."

"Awesome." Kick settled into her seat. "You know, I've never been to the historical society."

Carolina grimaced. "You're not missing much."

She's right again, Kick thought when they pulled into a weed-pocked parking lot. Located in a once-upon-a-time gas station, the Bohring Town Historical Society's glass doors were clouded with dirt, the Coca-Cola sign out front was riddled with bullet holes, and someone had backed over both gas pumps, leaving them to rust in the sun.

"Does everything in Bohring have to be creepy?" Kick asked as Uncle Freeport drove away. "I mean, *really.*"

"My house isn't creepy. We have gnomes."

"Yeah, about that . . ."

Carolina narrowed her eyes and soldiered toward the double doors. A sign with curled corners had been taped to the inside glass:

BOHRING TOWN HISTORICAL SOCIETY
OPEN DAILY

Kick rattled the door's handle. For a heartbeat, it held . . .

and then the door creaked open. Dusty air rushed out as the girls edged in.

Or rather, as Kick edged in.

Carolina stood in the doorway, looking around. She looked up. She looked down. She sniffed the air. Twice. "Maybe you have a point."

"What?"

"Everything in Bohring *is* creepy. I don't want to go in."

Technically, Kick wasn't sure she wanted to go in either. Where packs of candy and containers of oil would've once been stacked on shelves, there were now rows and rows of newspaper stacks and old books. Where a fan once hung from the ceiling, exposed wiring hung down. Shadows clotted in *all* the corners.

"It looks like a bomb went off," Kick whispered.

"It looks like a fire hazard."

And then one of the shadows *moved*.

"Who's there?" the shadow asked.

"Um," Kick managed, "us?"

"Who's 'us'?" The lowering sun through the window sent the shadow toward them, floating over the concrete floor until it transformed into a woman with fierce over-bright eyes and a halo of black hair. "I'm Mrs. Danvers. Who're you?"

"Kick Winter and Carolina Freeport."

"What do you want?"

"Um . . ." Kick glanced at Carolina and then back to Mrs. Danvers. "Mrs. Danvers, I'll be honest. I was hoping to find some information on the curse . . . you know . . . *the curse.*"

"Of course I know the curse. It's upon us even as we speak."

"Ah. Okay, well, could you help us?"

Mrs. Danvers's eyes narrowed. "You want me to help you find out how you'll eventually perish?"

Kick paused. "Yes?"

"Well, I suppose we all would if we could. This way." She waved for the girls to follow her. "Consider yourselves lucky. I'll have to wait to find out how I'll die."

"So lucky," Carolina muttered. "So very, very lucky."

Mrs. Danvers led them deeper into the shelves. Stacks of books and newspapers climbed toward the ceiling, blocking out some of the overhead lights and casting much of the floor in darkness. Mrs. Danvers tugged at some newspapers on her right and frowned, tugged at a book on her left and scowled. She tugged at a plastic milk crate and nearly brought an entire shelf down on them.

"Here," she said at last, dust swirling around her head. "These are what people usually want when they come looking for the curse."

She passed Kick the milk crate. Inside, there was a fat book and a thin book. Both their titles had been rubbed away long ago. "Thank you!"

But Mrs. Danvers had already swept away, her footsteps ricocheting into nothing. Kick frowned. "What'd I say?"

"You have that effect on people." Carolina shouldered ahead. "Which book do you want?"

"The thin one."

"Way to challenge yourself."

"I know. I like to think it's one of my better qualities." Kick opened the thin book and flipped to the title page.

A Study in Fear

"What is it?" Carolina asked, not looking up.

"Not sure. What's yours?"

"*History of Bohring.* Someone's turned down every page that mentions the witch."

Kick skimmed over the first few chapters of *A Study in Fear.* "Oh. Mine's about . . . mass hysteria or mass psychogenic disorder."

"Huh?"

"I'm not sure either." For several minutes, they both went quiet, reading. The fluorescent lights above them buzzed like wasps. "Okay, got it." Kick turned another page, still skimming. "Mass hysteria is where people believe in stuff that isn't happening. They have all these examples—like, in one case, people thought witches were making these girls hallucinate, but really it was the moldy bread everyone was eating."

"What?" Carolina grabbed the book from Kick. "Whoa. And there are also cases where peer pressure made people think they were sick or were all seeing stuff."

"Like monsters?"

"Sort of. They have some cases where people thought they were witnessing miracles—oh, and *smelling stuff*! It's just like what Mrs. Flagg said happened in Bohring."

Kick paused. What if the same thing was happening again? What if everyone thought the curse was real because they were feeding off each other? It made beautiful sense— until she remembered she'd also seen the lights and smelled the smell and she didn't believe in the curse at all.

"Any of that helpful?" Carolina asked, passing *A Study in Fear* back to Kick.

"Maybe. What about yours?"

Carolina looked down at her book. "The whole thing started with Mrs. Miller being accused of witchcraft."

Kick rolled her eyes so hard she should've been able to see her brain's frontal lobe. "There's no such thing as witch-craft."

Carolina flipped a page. "Yeah, but Mrs. Miller was probably eccentric, and you *know* how people act when somebody's different."

"Okay, so they accused her of witchcraft, and then what?"

"Then she cursed the town, and then people started smelling stuff and hearing things."

"Let me guess, and after that they saw the monsters?"

Carolina nodded. "Maybe that's mass hysteria too?"

"Could be—and now we know Cash and the message are aberrations. That's good."

"Sure, as long as you don't care how everyone's freaking out. . . ." Carolina hissed in a breath, still reading. "Oh my gosh, I didn't know about this. Last time this happened in Bohring, some of the kids *attacked* each other."

There was a shift behind them, a blink of light through the towers of books.

"I'm locking up for the night." Both girls jumped as Mrs. Danvers rounded the corner.

She's been listening the whole time, Kick realized, a chill settling over her. She clutched *A Study in Fear* to her chest.

"Did you find everything you needed?" Mrs. Danvers asked.

"Yes. Thank you."

"If you want to continue reading, you'll have to check that out. Sign the slip in the back and give it to me."

Hands gone clammy, Kick turned to the last page and found a paper pocket holding a checkout slip. She pulled it out, gaze running from borrower to borrower to . . . JBB.

"Jeremiah Butler Burr," Kick whispered. As in *Mayor* Jeremiah Butler Burr.

"Your story is about to take an interesting turn."

The mayor's signature was round and faded. *Old*, Kick realized, checking the dates next to the other signatures. At least thirty years old. Mayor Burr must've checked this out when he was a kid.

"What is it?" Carolina whispered.

"Look!" She tapped the name, keeping one eye on Mrs. Danvers. She'd gone behind a heavy wooden desk, had taken out a heavy register, and seemed to be having a serious argument with herself.

And she looked unhappy about it. Like she was losing.

Next to Kick, Carolina went still. Her eyes ran over and over Mayor Burr's swoopy handwriting. "But those initials would spell—"

"Are you checking those books out or not? If you are, come and sign for them." Mrs. Danvers paused, watching them. "What is it?"

Kick began to sweat. "Nothing."

"It's something."

"N-no," Carolina stammered. "It's nothing." She was going for Innocent Carolina, the one adults always adored, but Mrs. Danvers didn't look like she adored anything about either of them.

Kick grabbed Carolina's arm and hauled her up to the desk. They took out both books' checkout cards and set them down.

"Nice and clear," Mrs. Danvers said, passing Kick a pen and then flicking one finger at the closest slip. The front was full, so Kick flipped it over, dropping down to the last empty boxes.

And noticing the signature just above it: Jefferson Butler Burr.

Again, she realized. This time, the handwriting was newer. Narrower. It slanted across the signature box like the name was being stabbed. Kick traced the *J* and the *B* with her fingertip. *The sign-out date is only a month ago.*

"Kick?" Carolina ground her name through clenched teeth. "Can you sign for the nice lady?"

"Sorry. I— Sorry." She dashed down her name and passed the cards to Mrs. Danvers, who made a note in the register and gave her the books.

"Is that everything you need?" she asked them.

They nodded.

"Good. Now get out."

Like I need the encouragement, Kick thought as Mrs. Danvers hustled them through the historical society's front doors. She slammed them shut behind the girls, and the lock scraped shut.

Carolina scratched her bare arm. "So. Creepy."

In spite of everything, Kick caught herself smiling. "Think your dad will be here soon?"

"Hopefully. It depends on how much work he has at the greenhouse."

Kick blinked and then blinked again. "You did it again. You said *greenhouse.*"

"I meant shop."

"You *said* greenhouse."

"Fine. Whatever. It's only half a shop. The rest is a greenhouse. Dad used to be a plant scientist for the Larimore Corporation. He loved it and he really missed it, so he built the greenhouse to continue his research."

"I can't believe you've been holding back on this."

"Believe me, it's not interesting. It's just a bunch of regular old plants."

Kick paused. "If he loved his work so much, why'd he quit?"

"Dunno. Wish I did." Carolina's expression was troubled, and it turned even more troubled when she looked down at the books in her cousin's arms. "Kick?"

"Yeah?"

"Why would the mayor check out that *Study in Fear* book twice?"

"Maybe he forgot he already read it? Or maybe he was just doing research? He could've had the same idea that we did: Go back to the beginning."

"Yeah," Carolina said.

"And he *couldn't* have been behind the twins disappearing," Kick added. "I was there. I would've seen him."

Carolina swatted at the gnats circling them. "Unless you missed something."

It was possible and sometimes happened to the best of scientists, but Carolina's observation still annoyed Kick. Then Carolina squinted into the dying sunlight and said something that annoyed her even more: "Maybe everything isn't supposed to fit together neatly. Maybe it's not supposed to make sense."

"But it *has to*. Everything is *explainable*."

But they could both hear the panic edging into her voice. Thunder rumbled in the distance, promising a late-afternoon storm. They happened all the time in Bohring, but now Kick caught herself worrying about the Macon twins. Would they be dry?

Were they *safe*?

She searched the trees, seeing nothing, and then . . .

"Monsters," Carolina whispered, her suddenly icy

hand closing over Kick's. They watched, breath held, as two green glows wove through the trees. They didn't circle anywhere near the historical society. They headed east. Straight for town.

Again.

"Don't do anything by halves if you want to get away with it."

Kick and Carolina weren't the only people who saw the monsters. By the time Kick made it halfway through the schoolyard the next morning, she'd already heard about how they'd spent most of the night circling the town, growling and snarling. She'd also already heard about how the Macon twins' search party had doubled in size.

"I don't know why they're still looking," one fifth-grader said to another as everyone dragged toward their classrooms. Kick was stuck behind them, feeling like if her eyes rolled any farther back in her head, they'd stick. "They'd be better off putting out some bacon—or whatever monsters eat."

"So true," another agreed. "Maybe now that Sheriff Day and Deputy Patel are taking the curse seriously, Cash will come back to school."

"Unlikely. I heard his mother's moving them to Atlanta and—"

Kick frowned, swerving out of the crowd and into Mrs. Flagg's classroom. After that, the morning passed in blissful repetition: homeroom, class, lunch . . . well, almost.

"Attention, class!" Mrs. Flagg was grinning hard. "Before lunch begins, I have a surprise for you. Thanks to grant money secured for the school, Dr. Callahan was able to buy televisions for all the classrooms—"

Jefferson sat up straight. "To watch movies?"

"No." Mrs. Flagg laughed, and Kick noticed she was starting to sound a bit brittle. "Not exactly. Miss Welty's class has created a school announcement program. It'll be just like watching the news but *better*! Won't this be fun?"

Not at all, Kick thought, slouching lower in her seat. *You need to get out more.*

Fun would be lighting trinitrotoluene. Or making a pumpkin explode with some vinegar and baking soda. Fun could even be flipping Figgis's chicken cutlets super high so he leaped for them, but there was nothing fun about other sixth-graders talking about the sixth grade.

Or any grade, Kick thought.

Mrs. Flagg wheeled the television to the front of the class and turned it on. The screen blinked to life, eventually revealing a dark-haired boy with a sunburn holding a stack of papers with shaky hands.

"Are we on?" he asked someone. "Yeah? Oh!"

He faced the camera, running one hand over his

close-cropped hair. "Hello, hello, Bohring Elementary and Middle School! I'm Elwood Jones from Miss Welty's class, and I'm your host."

Kick vaguely recognized him. Did his mother come to the Hollows for readings? No, that wasn't it. Was it from the playground? Oh. Kick nodded to herself. He was the one who liked to squish ants.

"It's gonna be another hot one," Elwood continued, rustling his papers. "Sixth-grade history reports will be due at the end of the month, and the third-graders are eagerly preparing their life-cycle-of-plants posters. Keep an eye out in the hallway. I'm sure you'll see them soon."

Kick reached under her seat, hunting for her experiment notebook. Could someone die of boredom? It seemed distinctly possible. Her fingers brushed the spiral binding and—

Carolina gasped. "El-Elwood," she managed.

Kick looked at her. "What about him?"

Carolina jammed one finger in the television's direction. "Look!"

Kick looked. "Impossible," she breathed.

But clearly it wasn't, because Elwood wasn't Elwood. Elwood was a monster.

34

"Oh, it can always get worse. Always."

The Jennas screamed first, shooting up so hard and fast, their chairs overturned. Natalie May and Mia screamed second, so the Jennas screamed again.

Or maybe they were still screaming. Kick wasn't sure. She'd instinctively covered her ears, but she couldn't move an inch—and she couldn't look away from Elwood.

How was this happening? How was this *possible*?

Because that was definitely a monster on the screen.

Elwood now had leathery gray skin and sunken black eyes. He held the announcement papers with yellow-clawed fingers, and every time he grinned, a seam of needle-sharp teeth flashed at the camera.

"What on earth?" Mrs. Flagg rushed from student to student, trying to settle them. "What are you screaming about?"

"I don't want to be a monster!" Mia cried, putting both

hands over her face. Mrs. Flagg knelt, pulling the girl close. She looked from Mia to the television to the students—and then back to the television. Her jaw dropped.

"What *is that*?"

"It's a monster!" someone yelled. "It's happening! The curse is happening!"

"Aieeeee!" went everyone—and it was *everyone*. Kick could hear screams coming from up and down the hallway outside their classroom. The whole school had seen Elwood the monster.

"But how?" Kick looked at Carolina, but Carolina was still staring at Elwood. Honestly? Kick didn't blame her. Between the teeth and the skin, he was difficult to look away from. "Is it a costume?"

Carolina slowly shook her head. "How would he have had time to change?"

"There has to be a reasonable explanation here!" Mrs. Flagg bellowed. "Everyone, calm down!"

Everyone did not calm down. Everyone became more excited. The Jennas shrieked louder and cowered at the back of the room. Jefferson dove under his desk. Natalie May and Mia burst into tears, and Duke and Leonard ran for the door.

"Don't go out there!" Jenna Jane screamed. "The monsters are out there! Stay in here and barricade the door!"

"No way!" Duke yelled. "I'm running for it!"

"She's right!" Leonard yelled at the same time. "Don't go out there!"

Leonard grabbed Duke, and they went down in a flurry of legs and arms. Jenna Jane screamed some more. "Let me go!" Duke yelled, scrambling for the door handle. "I gotta get out of—"

Leonard swung his fist around, connecting with Duke's cheek. There was a sickening thump. It was horrible, but the sudden memory it brought back was almost as bad:

Last time this happened in Bohring, Carolina had said at the historical society, *some of the kids attacked each other.*

And now it was happening again. Kick grabbed Carolina's hand and held on.

"Knock it off!" Mrs. Flagg screamed, and leaped into the fray. She grabbed both boys by their shirts and hauled them apart.

Unsuccessfully.

Duke swung at Leonard, and Leonard kicked Duke in the knee.

Carolina gripped Kick's hand harder. "I've always wanted to kick Duke like that," she whispered. "Always."

"What?" But Kick didn't really care. Her attention had returned to the television and Elwood the monster. "This isn't right."

Carolina blinked. "Duh."

"No. It isn't *right.*" Kick leaped onto a desk chair,

hauling Carolina with her. Both of them narrowly avoided being stomped by Jefferson, who was dragging a bookshelf barricade toward the door.

"What's going on out there?" Elwood asked.

Kick froze, slowly turning toward the television. It was Elwood's voice and Elwood's image, but his mouth hadn't moved.

Actually . . . nothing had moved.

It's a trick, Kick realized about a half a second before she also realized Elwood looked back at her. *Elwood.* Not a monster.

But everyone was still screaming.

"Something changed," she breathed.

"Huh?" Carolina teetered on the desk chair. Her fingers dug hard into Kick's forearm as she tried to angle herself around without falling.

"Look!" Kick pointed.

Carolina looked, and all her breath left in a whoosh. "He's not a monster anymore."

Exactly, Kick thought, studying the floors and desks around them. Something had changed, but what? They were still standing in the same place. They were still facing the same direction. The temperature in the room hadn't changed. The light hadn't—

Wait a second. Her brain raced back to Mrs. Flagg's earlier confusion. *What on earth?* she'd said when it was pretty stinking obvious Elwood had gone monstrous.

Slowly, Kick stepped down from the desk chair. Immediately, Elwood the monster reappeared. He had the leathery skin, the sunken eyes, the *teeth*. Yeah, the picture didn't move, but it didn't have to. He was scary enough—and with the audio still coming through, it kinda seemed like the whole thing was live.

Still eyeing the image, Kick jumped back onto the chair. Elwood smeared back into Elwood.

"Height," she breathed, pulse pounding. "The image is affected by *height*. This is awesome!"

But it wasn't, because a book flew through the air and Carolina dove from the chair, colliding with Kick and taking them both to the floor.

"Monsters!" Leonard cried.

Kick peeked up, and while she knew Leonard usually sat two rows behind her and rarely said a word, she almost didn't recognize him. He didn't look the same. The glint in his eyes had turned him wild.

Monstrous.

"Trust no one. Well, no one except for me. That'll be another five dollars."

Outside, the shrieks climbed another octave, and Mrs. Flagg began to scream for everyone to sit down. *"Sit down!"*

Carolina wiggled around on her belly to look at Kick. *"Why?* Why would someone do this?"

"No idea."

"You need to tell Mrs. Flagg."

In unison, their gazes swung to the teacher, and Kick scowled. "Oh, yeah, because that won't look convenient at all. 'Gee, Mrs. Flagg, you know how I had a vision about the sensors? Well, gosh, now I've stumbled upon some weird blip with the televisions, but I had nothing to do with it. Promise.'"

"You're so annoying when you're right."

"Thank you?"

Another book hurtled through the air, and Carolina shot her cousin a desperate look. "We have to do something!"

"Fine!" Kick hurled herself to her feet, put both hands to her temples—because if ever there had been "a really hard question," now was it—and bellowed: "Mrs. Flagg! I'm having a vision!"

"Not! Now! Miss Winter!"

"The spirits want us to stand on our desks and see the truth!" Kick screamed, and she screamed it loud enough that her classmates actually stopped throwing things at each other.

And they stood on *their* desks.

"It isn't real," Jenna Jane said, sounding awed.

"Told you," Kick said, and then realized she was still holding her temples. She dropped her hands and tried to act casual. It didn't work. Sometimes there was simply no playing off a vision. "It's something to do with the . . . something. I have an article on it. Somewhere. At home."

Mrs. Flagg's nostrils flared as she inhaled. Hard. "Please sit down," she said, sounding faint.

"Yes. Please," Carolina added, also sounding faint.

Kick sat. So did everyone else. The television screen had gone black—someone must've turned off the feed—but shrieks still echoed through the school.

"I will be right back," Mrs. Flagg said. "Do not even *think* about moving." Then she pried the classroom door open and ran down the hallway, calling for Miss Welty.

Carolina yanked her chair so close the girls' knees

touched. "When I said you needed to tell Mrs. Flagg, I didn't mean you should have a vision!"

"Oh. Well. You should've been more specific."

The muscles in Carolina's jaw twitched once and then again. "*How* would someone do this?"

Kick frowned. She knew this one. She just couldn't quite remember it. "It's something about . . . the angles? I read it somewhere. I still have the article."

"Think it says why anyone would want to do this?"

"Doubtful." Down the hallway, the shrieks and screams quieted, replaced by soft sobbing. It was even worse. Kick squirmed. "We need to ask who benefits from this. If we figure that out, we'll have the culprit."

"And then what?"

Good question. Kick tried to picture herself explaining all of this to Sheriff Day or Deputy Patel, and, well, she couldn't. There were some things even a future super scientist couldn't envision. "I'll come up with something," she said at last. "I just need to get to my research."

***

And luckily for Kick, less than an hour later, she was about to get her chance. All the students were herded into the dusty schoolyard, and once the teachers got everyone to hush (or in the first-graders' case, to stop crying), Mayor Burr motioned for Principal Locke to make her announcement: "Due to unforeseen technical difficulties, Bohring

Elementary and Middle School will close for the rest of the day."

Going to have to remember that one, Kick thought as a gasp rolled over the schoolyard. Teachers trembled. Students whimpered. Everywhere she looked, fear looked back. *Due to unforeseen technical difficulties, I will be unable to clean my room.*

Or better yet: Due to unforeseen technical difficulties, I cannot be held responsible for a small fire.

Or a large fire.

"But worry not!" Mayor Burr cried, clapping a hand onto Principal Locke's shoulder with such force she staggered. "Bohring Elementary and Middle School will be open tomorrow!"

"Amazing how quickly he shows up," Carolina whispered, "isn't it?"

Kick paused. "The hardware store *is* pretty close." Sunshine beat down through the tree branches, and everyone huddled in patches of shade. She wanted to look at her cousin, but somehow she didn't dare. "It wouldn't take him long to get here."

"True," Carolina added under her breath. "And he is the mayor. People probably call him when something goes wrong."

Which was absolutely reasonable. So why didn't it feel right?

Kick frowned.

"Well," Principal Locke added, casting a worried glance in Mayor Burr's direction. "We might not be open tomorrow, but definitely the day after. Unless we can't get to the bottom of our electrical . . . glitch."

Going to have to remember that one too, Kick thought.

"Miss Bessy and Dr. Callahan are calling everyone's parents," Principal Locke continued. Her hands were folded in front of her chest, and her expression was serene—well, except for her twitching left eye. It matched Mrs. Flagg's. "You are not to leave until your parents arrive, and you are *not* to go anywhere alone. Do you understand?"

Everyone understood. Kick felt like she especially understood. The teachers were scared. The kids were scared. Aunt Aly was probably furious and Uncle Freeport was undoubtedly speeding toward the school, but because the speeding involved Flubber, it probably wasn't very speedy.

"And there's a town meeting tonight!" Mayor Burr bellowed, stepping ahead of Principal Locke. "Everyone is to meet back here by seven to discuss the situation—only, it isn't a *situation*, because I'm handling everything!"

Kick sat on the steps, Carolina next to her, and they both watched Jefferson sell more pennies as his dad continued to bellow about how everything was under control. Jefferson's line was four students deep now, and they just kept coming. Kick nudged her cousin. "You sure he isn't behind this?"

Carolina frowned, studying Jefferson. After a moment, she shook her head. "I don't think so. When Elwood turned into a monster, Jefferson was just as scared as the rest of us. I saw him."

"Maybe he's a good actor?"

"Maybe." But Carolina didn't sound like she believed it.

"There's nothing to worry about, though," Principal Locke added. "I will see all of you soon—"

"Unless the curse gets you first!"

Someone gasped. Kick turned. The crowd turned. The Macon boys—filthy and furious—stomped into the schoolyard.

Buford Macon led the way, but Buddy Macon shouldered ahead and said, "Because the curse isn't coming! It's already here, and we're all doomed!"

GRANDMA MISSOURI'S
PREDICTION

36

"People are frightened, illogical, and selfish. Do right by them anyway."

"The curse is on us," Buddy Macon said, pushing a wet—and filthy—hunk of hair from his eyes. "We smelled the smell, and we heard the monsters coming for us. We had no choice but to take off."

"And get lost," Buford added.

"It wasn't intentional."

"I bet they know that."

"I bet they don't."

And after that, Kick couldn't hear a thing. Parents hurried through the spiny, spiky gate and started yelling. Students who were in the dusty schoolyard began hollering back. And the mayor was yelling and hollering louder than everyone.

"Where have you *been*?" he bellowed, face going a horrible shade of purple.

A man standing behind the twins waved. He looked, as

Grandma Missouri would say, as if he'd stuck his tongue in a toaster: His white hair stood straight up and his thin face was flushed.

"Terribly sorry about that, Burr," he said. "The boys were with me, and I don't have a phone and—" He broke off into a peal of slightly creepy laughter. "Why would I have a phone anyway? It's not like the alligators would call me, now is it? No, indeed. No, sir."

Carolina slapped one hand over her eyes and shook her head.

"What is it?" Kick hissed.

"That's Dr. Hazmat." Her cousin didn't look up. "He's this billionaire recluse alligator researcher weirdo who lives in the swamp. Dad knows him."

"Wow. Only in Bohring."

"Pretty much."

Kick rocked onto her toes, looking around. She caught Mia watching her. The other girl's cheeks pinkened, and she turned away.

"They're not talking to you anymore, are they?" Carolina asked.

"No, but they will as soon as I get this curse stuff handled. We'll be friends again."

"Were they really your friends to begin with? You weren't . . . *you* around them. You should let people see the real you. Explosions and all."

"I've tried that. Nobody wants to be around that girl. I was alone all the time."

"I'd rather be alone than be with people who make me feel alone."

Kick looked at her cousin and felt another piece of her had fallen into place. Maybe Carolina wasn't alone all the time because she had to be, but because she chose to be.

"There's Dad," Carolina said, hopping up and dusting off her skirt. "Let's go."

They wove through the mob, dodging students and parents, to get to Flubber. The mint-colored car backfired. It almost sounded like a hello.

"Are you two okay?" Uncle Freeport asked as they climbed in. "I don't understand what happened. A monster appeared on television?"

"Something like that," Carolina said. "It was really weird. When we stood on the floor, Elwood looked just like a monster, but when we stood on a chair, he was Elwood again."

Uncle Freeport turned to look at them. "Did you figure that out?"

"Kick did."

His eyes went to Kick. She could feel heat climb her face, but she tried to keep her expression bored, like she made discoveries all the time and maybe he should rethink his No Kick in the Shop/Greenhouse stance.

"*Technically,*" she said at last, "I was trying to keep Carolina and me from getting squished by Jefferson Burr and climbed on a desk chair. Then I noticed the difference. Not really the same as figuring it out properly."

Uncle Freeport shrugged. "That's okay. Observation is the first step in the scientific method. Plus, most scientists stand on the shoulders of their predecessors."

"Oh." She thought about that. "I stood on a chair."

Uncle Freeport shook his head. "It's a proverb," he explained.

"What?"

"A proverb," Carolina said, massaging her forehead with one hand. "Like 'necessity is the mother of invention.'"

"Hardly," Kick said. *Boredom* is the mother of invention. That's when I get my best ideas."

"Define 'best,'" Carolina said.

"Well," Uncle Freeport said, "chairs or shoulders, you two have had quite a morning. That explanation makes more sense, I guess. Your mother's beyond furious," he added, glancing up in the rearview mirror at Carolina. "She's on the phone with the school superintendent now. You can imagine how that's going."

Carolina winced. "It's only going to get worse. Guess who showed up to say the curse is real? The Macon twins."

"Are you sure? You saw them? They're *safe*?"

"As far as I can tell, Dr. Hazmat brought them back. They'd been staying with him."

"*Seriously!*"

Kick perked up. "Is he that bad?"

"No. No, no. He's just . . . eccentric. He's very passionate about his work."

"That's a nice way of saying he prefers alligators to people," Carolina told her, and before her father could object, added, "The mayor's called a town meeting for tonight, and the twins are saying the curse is here and we're all doomed."

"Well, I guess the positive takeaway is that they're okay." Uncle Freeport steered Flubber into the increasing traffic. Flubber backfired. "But there has to be a better explanation for this. Way better."

"That's what I've been saying," Kick told him. But her uncle wasn't listening. He shook his hands loose from their death grip on the steering wheel and patted the car's dash like it was a stubborn pony. "I need to get back to the shop immediately and—"

Kick brightened. "Oh, good, we could come help you."

"Not going to happen. I don't want you two anywhere near town. I'm taking both of you straight to Grandma Missouri's. I'll pick you up when I'm done, Carolina, okay?" His eyes lifted to the rearview mirror again.

Carolina nodded, but she didn't look any more excited

about it than Kick was. Uncle Freeport seemed lost in his own thoughts. It would've been a silent ride to the Hollows if it weren't for the traffic flying past them.

The long dirt road was usually empty, but today cars passed them coming *from* the Hollows and cars passed them going *to* the Hollows. Some roared by. Some rumbled. One truck had crates of chickens packed into the bed. Feathers flew everywhere.

Uncle Freeport turned on his windshield wipers. "Looks like your grandma is busy today." They came around the last turn for the Hollows, and he loosed a low whistle. "Looks like your grandma is *very* busy today."

The girls leaned forward, hanging over his seat to see. Cars and trucks lined the grass on either side of the long dirt road. They were parked by the Hollows' gate and by the fence. In some places, they were three deep. In others, they were bumper to bumper.

"There must be twenty cars," Kick muttered.

"Way more than twenty." Carolina turned to her father. "Why can't we stay at our house?"

"Because your mother's working and I need to get back to the shop. I don't want you two alone right now. The town isn't right."

Looking at the people waiting outside the Hollows, Kick agreed. Jolene Jones—the woman from the schoolyard with eyebrows like bottlebrushes—was there, arguing with

Mr. Jessup. Earl stood right behind both of them, egging on Jolene, and a man with a wrestling T-shirt tucked into his sweatpants watched the whole thing like it was fascinating. Even from here, Kick could see his belly button pushing through the T-shirt, like it was trying to escape.

"They'll clear out soon," Uncle Freeport continued, slowing Flubber to a stop. "Everyone will head into town for the mayor's meeting."

Everyone didn't look like they were heading anywhere, but Kick let it go. "C'mon," she said to Carolina.

They slid out of Flubber and made their way down the crooked path, weaving between grown-ups.

"I need a charm," one woman told Carolina, catching her shoulder as they tried to pass. "I need it *now*."

Carolina gaped. "Uh . . ."

"What do you mean 'uh'? Don't you have some of these things already prepared?"

"Uh . . ."

"You'll have to wait your turn," Kick said, dragging her cousin away. "Shouldn't she know that? That's like kindergarten stuff."

Carolina shrugged. "I don't know. Elwood still hasn't learned it."

"That's *Elwood's* mom?"

She nodded. "And that's Mia's mom, and that's Jenna B.'s dad."

Kick's center sank. It looked like the grown-ups were just as scared as the kids—and they were arguing like kids too, their voices climbing.

But one voice climbed above everyone's: "This town's always had a curse," Mr. Jessup told Jolene, wagging his finger to make his point. "And you know who benefits from it? Missouri. That's who."

37

"Beware of those closest to you."

Kick gaped. Mr. Jessup had known Grandma Missouri for years. They were *friends*!

And now he was turning on her—worse, other people were starting to listen to him.

"Think about it," he continued, "who's making money off all this? Who could make something like this happen?" His watery blue eyes roamed from face to face until they landed on the cousins.

"Well, for starters—" Kick began.

Carolina dragged her up the front porch steps. "Forget it," she whispered.

"How?" Mr. Jessup's words had wrapped around Kick's heart like they belonged to her. "It's true. She does benefit. We can't pick and choose our data."

"She would never hurt people like that." Carolina shoved the front door open—or tried to shove it open.

Inside the cottage was just as crowded as outside the cottage, and the door crashed into a waiting customer. The woman *tsk*ed at them. "Sorry, Mrs. Omoto," Carolina said, squeezing past. "You *know* she wouldn't," she whispered to Kick.

"Of course I do. But Mr. Jessup is telling everyone in line. How long until they believe him?"

"I don't know. Not long?"

"Then what happens?" In movies, angry townspeople liked to attack villains with pitchforks and torches. Kick didn't know if Bohring townspeople would resort to the same measures, but it did seem like something they would enjoy.

Bing! Biiinnnggg! The front door tried to swing open again as more people wedged themselves into the Hollows' tiny foyer. Someone stumbled into Cecil. The stuffed bear wobbled dangerously, his deerstalker cap falling off.

Kick grabbed Carolina's hand and shoved her way to the staircase. "C'mon. If we're going to get to the bottom of this, I need my research."

***

It's around here somewhere, Kick thought moments later as she checked her bedroom's overcrowded bookshelves. Unfortunately, there was no sign of the three-ring binder.

"Don't you ever clean?" Carolina asked, toeing a pair of dirty coveralls. Kick paused, trying to see the bedroom with fresh eyes. There was her tiny bed (unmade), her tiny desk (cluttered), and her pile of laundry (mountainous) tossed next to the closet. It did look a bit . . . untidy.

"The floor is the biggest shelf you own. I'm simply making better use of it." Kick tossed dirty laundry away from the closet and whipped the doors open. That research was around here *somewhere.*

Under the bedroom lights, her chemistry set's beakers glistened satisfyingly. Yes, the ironing board was flowery and undignified, but her glow-in-the-dark slime?

Well, okay. That was fairly undignified as well. It wasn't slime anymore. It had dried out. With all the excitement about curses and monsters, Kick had forgotten it entirely.

Pretty much like she'd forgotten she wasn't supposed to be practicing chemistry.

"Tell me that's not what I think it is," Carolina said.

Slowly, Kick turned. "You can't say anything."

No response.

"Carolina, I mean it. You can't tell Grandma Missouri."

"I'll think about it." She paused. "What's with the bags of sand?"

"*What?* Oh. Um, they're for an experiment to create liquid sand. I think it'll work like quicksand, and since I can't actually *get* quicksand, it'll have to do."

"I'm probably going to regret asking this, but why would you want to do that?"

"I think the better question is why *wouldn't* I?" Kick flung herself into the closet and started throwing things out.

Out went a box of fishing line.

Out went a handful of *Scientific American*s.

Out went another handful of *Scientific American*s.

She paused, mid-throw, to inspect a box of squirrel clothes. One of the squirrel dresses precisely matched one of Kick's (few) dresses. She wasn't sure how she felt about that. Creeped out seemed a bit excessive, but also applicable. She shoved the box to one side as Carolina's shadow fell over her.

"You need your *what*?" she asked.

"Research clippings. You know ... clippings of research."

"I know what—"

"Here they are!" Kick popped to her feet, clutching a three-ring binder to her chest. It was deliciously heavy. "I cut out interesting articles and put them in here."

"Like scrapbooking."

"No. Not like scrapbooking."

"Yes, like scrapbooking. In fact, that's pretty much *entirely* scrapbooking."

Kick ignored her. She dropped to her knees on the rug and began flipping through the plastic-coated pages. "I know I've seen that television thing before," she said aloud to herself, passing an article about alien cover-ups ("Ridiculous."), an editorial about a weather machine that could be used as a weapon ("Fascinating."), and a set of directions for turning kitty litter into napalm ("Haven't had a chance to try it. Yet.").

"It was something about an electronic screen," she said. "It revealed two different images—not monsters, obviously."

"Obviously." Carolina was looking—and failing—to find a clean place to sit down. In the end, she had to kneel on the *Scientific American*s and hold very still so nothing else touched her.

"Was it a sign?" Kick paused to peer closer at an article about cloning, not because it had anything to do with what she was looking for, but because it was interesting. "Notice board?"

"Like they use for advertisements?"

"*Yes!* An advertisement! *That's* what it was!" She flipped, flipped, and found it: an article about electronic signage in London, England. It had been designed to reach children who were being abused. From a high angle, like the height of an adult, it looked like a regular advertisement with a kid. From a low angle, like the height of a kid, it showed a help-hotline number.

She tapped her fingertip to the glossy page. "And *this* is why you never throw anything away."

"Please." Her cousin looked around the bedroom in disgust. "This is also how you get typhoid."

"No, it's not. Actually—"

Carolina gestured for Kick to pass her the binder. "Give it to me. I want to read too."

"Fine." She waited, vibrating, until Carolina finished the article.

"Huh." Her cousin's eyes snaked back and forth and back and forth like she was reading the same sentence again and again. "So, images can look different when seen from varying heights."

"Which is why we could only see Elwood's real face when we stood on the desks. Anyone under five foot four wouldn't see it. They would only see a monster. It also must be why the live feed stopped. They needed a static image. It's a trick, not a curse."

"But someone *is* using the curse. Why?"

Kick shrugged. "Grandma Missouri says everyone needs a shtick."

"Yeah, well, she also says ketchup is basically tomato sauce and puts it on spaghetti."

This was true, and gross, but Kick was too busy thinking about how everyone did need a shtick: Grandma Missouri was the town psychic, Mayor Burr wanted to be seen as the town's hero, and Jefferson was the lucky-penny kid.

"Maybe it *is* Jefferson," Kick said slowly. "He could've gotten the doorbell sensors from his dad's hardware shop, stolen Mrs. Flagg's key, and made a copy."

"But how would he have made the monsters?"

"The growls could be recordings? Maybe the stench is being released via fans?"

But the explanations were weak, and both girls knew it. Carolina frowned. "And the glowing?"

"Easy. Fluorescent paint. You can buy it or make it."

Carolina's frown deepened. "It makes better sense if it were Jefferson's dad. He's up for reelection. He needs to look good—and what would look better than creating a problem he gets to solve?"

Kick started to say that was impossible, but the more she thought about the idea, the more it stuck.

"Let's write it out." She went to the whiteboard hung on her wall. There were complicated formulas written all over it—not real, of course—but Kick liked the look of them and she couldn't wait for the day she would finally understand why anyone would want to put letters in math.

She picked her favorite blue marker, wiped away a patch of whiteboard, and wrote a number one. "One, the mayor owns the hardware store that sells doorbell sensors. Two, we see him at school all the time and he can probably go anywhere because he's the mayor. And three, fluorescent paint is easy to come by."

But it didn't explain how he created the growls, smells, or monster on the television. She tapped the marker against her chin. "Didn't Mrs. Flagg say Dr. Callahan got us those televisions? A grant or something?"

Carolina straightened. "Yeah, and she *does* have access to the classroom and she *could've* bought the paint and doorbell sensors. But why would she do it? She's all about helping and feelings."

"Maybe she wanted everyone to come to her for counseling?"

"Do you hear yourself?"

Honestly? Kick did, and it was annoying. She was stretching for answers.

"It's the mayor," Carolina said, nodding. "Maybe we don't know all the details on *how* yet, but we have the *why*: He wants to look like a hero so he gets reelected."

Kick took a shaky breath. "So what's he willing to do next?"

GRANDMA MISSOURI'S PREDICTION

"All is not as it seems."

How was it possible for things to keep getting worse? Kick wasn't sure. This seemed like an excellent potential experiment ("How bad can things get? No, *really*."), but also a frightening one.

Bing! Biiinnnggg!

Carolina winced as the doorbell erupted again. "Why doesn't she turn that off?"

"It's wired to the table-shaker." Kick tapped the marker to her chin, still studying the whiteboard. "If you turn one off, you turn them both off. Good for our ears, not good for business. I'm hungry," she added, dropping the marker into the whiteboard's tray.

"How can you eat at a time like this?"

"Easily. I like to think of it as another one of my better qualities."

Carolina pressed two fingers to her left eye. "Fine. Whatever."

"Good. Let's go."

Easier said than done, of course. The line of customers downstairs hadn't diminished, and the air felt solid, a mix of heat and sweat and someone's oversweet perfume.

Kick dragged Carolina past the last few grown-ups, grabbed Cecil's rather-trampled deerstalker cap from the floor, and ducked into the yellow kitchen. Thanks to the hastily fixed hole in the floor, it smelled like swamp, and thanks to Grandma Missouri's breakfast, the swamp had undernotes of bacon.

"So let me get this straight," Carolina said, pulling out silverware and arranging it in mismatched silvery stripes. "We're going to accuse Mayor Burr of being behind the curse?"

"Is it accusing when you know you're right?" Kick went to the refrigerator. It took a couple tries to see what they had, since Grandma Missouri liked to reuse margarine containers ("It's free Tupperware, child!"), but after a moment, she found some homemade pimento cheese. "Cheese sandwich?"

"Sure."

"You get the bread. I'll get the plates."

Kick went to the cupboard while Carolina got out a loaf of Wonder Bread. Yellow sunlight pooled on the Formica countertops, curling into small circles like a sleepy cat. It almost felt homey, making sandwiches with her cousin, hanging out in the kitchen.

As long as homey also included brainstorming ways to catch a disturbed politician determined to gain reelection via doorbell sensors and fluorescent paint.

Probably took him forever to smear the paint on his monsters too, Kick thought, feeling smug until the idea had a moment to circle around in her brain. She couldn't picture Mayor Burr doing anything so . . . messy. And more importantly, wasn't most of that paint toxic? It would've made his monsters sick.

Kick's fingertips began to tingle. Something wasn't right here. Carolina was right. She *had* missed something, but it wasn't from the swamp. "Do you still have the books from the historical society?"

"Of course, I do. Because guess which one of us is responsible?" Her cousin grabbed her backpack off the table and fished around. She started to pass Kick both books and paused. "Why do you look like you're about to throw up?"

"I don't think our theory works."

"What? We *just* went over this."

"But that was before I thought about the monsters in the swamp. He would've had to cover them in paint. I just can't see him doing it. Plus, a lot of that paint is toxic. It would've poisoned his monsters."

The girls went quiet, and then Carolina straightened. "Bioluminescence."

For five whole heartbeats, Kick was confused, and

then suddenly Uncle Freeport's impromptu biology lesson came rushing back: Certain plants glowed, and if you used those plants, you could make glowing paint. "Do you think Mayor Burr's capable of it?"

"You think anyone else is?"

"Actually . . ." Kick reached for the books still clasped in Carolina's arms. She opened *A Study in Fear* to the last page. Just like before, names were scrawled up and down the card. Just like before, JBB was the last entry. "Who else could JBB be?"

Carolina considered it. "I don't know, but I also don't know who AG is or MC or—"

"Wait a minute." Kick's fingertips began to tingle again. What had Mrs. Flagg called Dr. Callahan this morning? Melinda. "MC. That's Melinda Callahan."

"Or Miss Cleo."

"I'll give you a minute to think about that one."

Carolina wrinkled her nose. "How do you know her first name's Melinda?"

"Mrs. Flagg used it this morning! I forgot. With everything going on, it didn't seem important and now—you know what this means, right? She could've bought the doorbell sensors. She could have a key to Mrs. Flagg's class. She would even know about bioluminescent paint because she has a doctorate in biology!"

"Mrs. Flagg mention that this morning too?"

"Grandma Missouri found out." Kick flipped the bread slices onto paper plates and jammed the knife deep into the pimento cheese. "She told Dr. Callahan she wasn't living up to what the universe wanted for her, and Dr. Callahan said she was doing just fine since she had dual doctorates in biology and psychology. We *have* to investigate her. Today. Right now."

Carolina crammed a handful of potato chips into her mouth, crunched meditatively, and then said, "I'm sorry. I think I just had an apoplectic fit. Did you just say you wanted to go investigate *Dr. Callahan*?"

"That's not how apoplectic fits work, and yes, I did."

"Oh, yeah?" Carolina lifted her chin. "Well, if that's not how they work, then how *do* they work?"

Kick smeared pimento cheese on a bread slice. She had no idea.

"That's what I thought."

"Regardless, we need to get ahead of this—and today? Today is the perfect opportunity."

Carolina stuffed another handful of chips in her mouth. True, she didn't object any further, but Kick thought she was chewing rather . . . aggressively.

"You know I'm right," Kick continued, finishing a second sandwich. "It really is the perfect opportunity. Grandma Missouri's so busy she'll never miss us."

Carolina chewed harder. "And we're going to get there *how*?"

"You can't walk?"

"Please. Of course I can walk. I even know a shortcut through the swamp. *But*"—her cousin grabbed one of the sandwiches and took a ferocious bite; it was even scarier than watching her eat chips—"we're supposed to stay put."

Kick glanced at the clock hanging over the kitchen door. It was barely past noon. "If we hurry, they'll never know we were gone."

Her cousin hesitated. She opened her mouth, and—

Grandma Missouri banged through the kitchen door. She was full-on Hollywood glamour today with a slinky red dress, perfect curls, and elbow-length white satin gloves. "Christmas has come early, girls. I need newt eyes. *Now.*"

Carolina made a gurgling noise as Kick hopped off the kitchen stool. She passed her grandmother her sandwich and went to the refrigerator. "How many do you need?" she asked, rummaging through the produce drawer for the container of peeled mini grapes. They weren't exactly newt eyes—okay, they weren't newt eyes at all—but if someone insisted on touching them, they would feel close enough.

"Going to need all of them." Grandma Missouri took two bites of Kick's sandwich and then one more. "And any adder tongues you can find."

"You mean the Twizzlers I cut up to look like adder tongues?" Kick asked.

"You're a very literal child, do you know that?"

Kick shrugged and passed Grandma Missouri the adder tongues that were really Twizzlers, and Grandma Missouri passed her back the sandwich. She held the Twizzlers' plastic baggie up to the kitchen light, inspecting her granddaughter's work, and nodded. "Nicely done, Kick."

"I thought so."

And with a bright white grin, Grandma Missouri swept out of the kitchen. For a moment, Kick and Carolina chewed their sandwiches in silence, and then the moment was done.

Bing! Biiinnnggg!

"Let me put it another way," Kick said, leaning toward Carolina. "If this turns out to be bioluminescent paint, Sheriff Day is going to be on the hunt, and who has a greenhouse that could grow bioluminescent plants? Who would even know *how* to grow bioluminescent plants?"

Carolina took a shaky breath. "My dad."

"You are about to embark on a dangerous journey."

Dr. Callahan lived on the very edge of town where the pot-holed black pavement met the potholed dirt road. Like the Hollows, her place was a tiny cottage with a wraparound porch and sun-faded paint. Unlike the Hollows, it lacked alligators, Christmas lights, and that certain Grandma Missouri flair.

But it *did* have a nice flowered wreath pinned to the front door.

And a greenhouse, Kick thought, studying the yard from behind the weeds that lined the long, dusty dirt road. "I can't believe I never noticed this before," she told Carolina.

"It's because you're always staring at the turnoff for Dad's garage."

This was true. You couldn't see the garage from the long, dusty dirt road, but that didn't stop Kick from staring at the turn every time they passed it. "Well, yeah, there's that, and for the record, you should have told me our school psychologist had a suspicious greenhouse."

"I would say I didn't have any way of knowing it was suspicious, but I won't because I'm not listening," Carolina told her, flicking an ant from her sleeve. "I'm too busy."

"Busy doing what?"

"Waiting for our opportunity."

Which, at the rate things were going, might never come. Unfortunately for the girls, Dr. Callahan was home and busy outside, planting flowers in the hanging baskets that swung from her porch rafters.

"We need to get back soon." Kick glanced down the long, dusty road that (eventually) led to the Hollows.

"I know. Maybe she'll leave for the town meeting?"

But Dr. Callahan didn't seem like she was in any hurry. She tucked pink flowers into green baskets, wiped sweat from her face, and, in general, seemed like she could stay there all day. Kick couldn't. Not only was there the whole "getting back to the Hollows before Grandma Missouri found out they were gone," but she also had ants tunneling into her sneakers.

"Oh please, oh please, oh please," she whispered, scratching at her ankles.

And as if Dr. Callahan had somehow heard the prayers, she carried her hat, gloves, and flowerpots around the back of the house.

Kick's heart filled her throat. They were alone. The front yard was deserted. Their chance was *here*.

"Not it," Carolina said.

"But—"

"You know the rules."

Kick did indeed. Scowling at her cousin, she stood and looked up and down the road. Nothing. No one. She looked at Dr. Callahan's house. Nothing. No one.

Or at least nothing and no one as far as Kick could see.

*But what if someone or some*thing's *there?* she wondered.

Carolina groaned and grabbed Kick's hand, dragging her across the dusty dirt road. They ducked through Dr. Callahan's garden gate and skirted around the side of the house. Crickets trilled in the pine trees that led down to the swamp. Kick caught herself watching the shadows curdle under them, watching and watching and watching—

And missing the dogs watching *her* through Dr. Callahan's windows.

Grrrrrr!

They hit the glass with a hard thump, and she reeled backward, almost falling. Carolina caught her. White spittle and smashed faces hit the clear glass.

"Dogs," Kick breathed.

"No kidding, Sherlock."

"No! *Dogs!*" Kick struggled to her feet, feeling as if her mind was finally settling. The monsters had run through the swamp on four legs.

With smashed-in faces.

Just like *these* dogs.

They'd splashed through the water and leaped over fallen branches. Shaggy, muddy hair had whipped around their wrinkled snouts. Every breath had been a snarl.

"The monsters were dressed-up dogs!" Kick grabbed Carolina. "It'd be easy to bathe them after they'd been in the swamp—you could even train them where to run!"

"And teach them to growl on command."

"And make them . . . glow."

Slowly—breathlessly—the girls turned toward the greenhouse. Carolina's voice was ground down to a wisp, when she managed: "If bioluminescent flowers are in there, what do we do?"

"Figure it out." And Kick forced herself forward. *How bad do you want to know?* she asked herself, and once again, it helped.

But she couldn't stop the cold sweat rolling underneath her clothes.

Thanks to the lowering sun, they were dipped in shade, but the greenhouse's doorknob was still warm when Kick grabbed it.

And it turned easily in her hand.

The door yawned open, and a million smells climbed up into the girls' noses: oversweet flowers, wet earth, water.

And something else.

Something . . . *rotten.*

Kick inhaled hard, feeling bile prick the back of her mouth. "I smell monsters."

"So do I." Carolina cast a glance behind them. "Hurry up!"

"I *am!*" But Kick could barely move, her legs felt Play-Doh floppy. The greenhouse wasn't that large, but it was magnificently organized, so many plants fitted into rows and rows of plastic containers. Everywhere Kick looked, something magnificent looked back:

Black dahlias the size of her head.

Vivid green vines as thick as her wrists.

Red lilies with thorns as sharp as the lilies were beautiful. Their silky petals looked bloody in the sunlight, and there were buckets of them. Buckets and *buckets*.

Carolina swallowed. "I know that flower."

"You do?"

"Yeah. *Smell*."

But Kick didn't have to smell to know what was waiting. What had the twins called the stench? Like a porta potty in August or rotten eggs—and when she leaned down and breathed in, she had to agree.

"That's awful."

"*That's* what monsters smell like." Carolina took the delicate stem between her thumb and forefinger. "It's called Ambitien. It's one of Dad's inventions." And she snapped it from its roots, holding it close until bright tears crowded her eyes. "I don't know why he left the Larimore

Corporation, but I know it had something to do with this."

Which was worrisome enough, but the more Kick looked around, the more she saw the scary behind the amazing: Heaps of Ambitien lilies waited next to laboratory-grade grinders and glass jars. Some of the flowers had already been ground up and the powder was being heated over low-lit burners, dissolving into red liquid. Dozens of bottles were already filled with it.

So much *Ambitien,* Kick thought. If she blew it into the air, she'd be blinded. If she drank it, she'd drown. "Why would Dr. Callahan need all this?"

"I don't know. It can't be good. What do we do?"

A voice rose up from somewhere outside the green-house. "Hello? Is someone there?"

Okay, Kick thought. *That's a little worrisome.* Or maybe more than a little worrisome because the more she loooked around, the more she saw the *scary* behind the amazing.

"Run!" Kick whispered, yanking Carolina's arm. And they did. They ran past the gorgeous huge dahlias and thick vines, galloped through the greenhouse door. Kick shut it behind them.

Well, *slammed* it behind them.

The cousins ran for the dusty dirt road, Carolina still clutching the lily tight to her chest. They burst through the garden gate, pounded across the road, and hurled themselves into the weeds.

Just as Dr. Callahan rounded the corner.

"I can't look," Carolina whispered.

"I can." In fact, Kick couldn't stop herself. She wiggled around on her belly and peered through the curtain of weeds, watching as Dr. Callahan strode into her front yard. She looked right. . . . She looked left. . . . She walked straight to the greenhouse and opened the door, peering inside.

Then she whipped around. "I know you're here!"

Carolina peeked through two fingers. "She knows we're *close.*"

"Shhh!"

"I can't. I'm going to pass out. If she finds us, we're dead. If she—"

"She's not going to find us." But Kick grabbed Carolina's hand and squeezed it because Carolina was right. If Dr. Callahan found them, they probably would be dead because the school psychologist looked furious.

She turned and turned, studying the trees and the road and swamp. She lifted one hand to her eyes, shielding them from the sun, and looked up and down the dusty dirt road and back and forth across her pretty yard.

But she didn't look behind the weeds across the road, and when she finally gave up and went inside, Carolina and Kick *ran.*

"Good luck is about to find you."

But they only made it fifty yards—maybe less—before Flubber appeared on the horizon. It was going the fastest Kick had ever seen it go. Dust swirled around the mint-colored car, blending with the black-smoke backfire.

"It's been nice knowing you," Carolina said faintly. "If you touch my Princess Posey stuff while I'm grounded, I will tell everyone about your closet laboratory—*and* I'll torch your *Scientific American*s. Do you understand?"

"I do." And Kick did—she really, *really* did—because even from here, she could tell Uncle Freeport had Serious Consequences on the brain. He skidded Flubber to a stop, dust wreathing around the tires, and launched himself from the driver's seat.

"Did you really think Missouri wouldn't notice you were gone?"

"Well . . . yeah." Kick scratched the back of her neck.

"We wouldn't have left if we'd thought she would."

The vein in Uncle Freeport's forehead bulged. "Boarding school," he muttered to himself. "Boarding school would fix this."

Or maybe the flower would, Kick thought. "Show him, Carolina." She pointed to her cousin, and after the briefest hesitation, Carolina lifted the lily for everyone to see. The petals were still a raw red, and even a few feet away, Kick could smell their awful stench.

Uncle Freeport shuddered. "That's Ambitien."

"I know." Carolina nodded, turning the lily around and around in her fingers.

"Where did you get it?"

Kick drew a small circle in the dirt with the toe of her sneaker. "We found it?"

"You found it." Uncle Freeport's eyes had gone huge, and the vein in his forehead was throbbing steadily now. *"Where?"*

"Dr. Callahan's greenhouse."

The vein throbbed harder. "Did she *see* you?"

"No." Kick started to add that that was because they were really good at sneaking around, but now didn't seem the time.

"It's what's behind the curse, isn't it?" Carolina asked.

"I don't kn— Well, some of it. Yes." Uncle Freeport shook his head as if trying to clear it. "I don't know what happened to Cash. That's separate. Or maybe connected. I haven't been able to figure it out yet."

"What *have* you figured out?" Kick asked, alarm and excitement leaping side by side in her chest until they felt the same.

Uncle Freeport paused, something tired and old crossing his face. "I developed Ambitien from the titan arum—"

"The what?" Kick asked.

"The corpse flower and—"

"Wait. *Corpse* like *body*?"

"Yes." The muscles in Uncle Freeport's jaw jumped. "It's famous for its beautiful blooms and its horrific stench, but I wasn't interested in that. My focus has always been on helping people, and this project was supposed to create plants whose properties would reduce anxiety. We created a hybrid, splicing and altering the DNA of several plants to create Ambitien. One of the side effects was bioluminescence. But depending on the preparation, it was also known to make subjects highly suggestible. Basically, they became mindless zombies who would agree to anything. I wanted nothing more to do with the project, but the company disagreed. They knew they could use it."

"Is that why you left?" Carolina whispered.

He nodded. "For me, science was always about helping humanity. This wouldn't."

Carolina and Uncle Freeport stared at each other like

they were the only two people on the road, which would have been annoying had Kick realized it. She hadn't, though. Her mind was too busy skipping back to Dr. Callahan's greenhouse.

Ambitien's effects depend on how it's prepared, she thought, feeling as if her spinning brain had suddenly slowed. Paused. "Like when the flower's ground into powder and cooked over low heat?"

Her uncle tensed. "Yes. If it's been combined with the right ingredients, it can make subjects docile and suggestible to anything—too much and they never come out of their trance."

Kick's heart double-thumped. "How much would you need to do that?"

"Not much." Uncle Freeport frowned. *"Why?"*

"Because Dr. Callahan has a *boatload.*" Which Kick knew was not a technical term—and Kick did love technical terms—but it was the only way to describe the piles and piles of powder waiting in the greenhouse.

For a second, Uncle Freeport swayed. "That's . . . *really* not good."

Pow! Something exploded inside Flubber, and Uncle Freeport cursed. He stomped around to the hood and opened it. Smoke poured out. "Must've overheated—" His eyes lifted, catching on something approaching in the distance.

Something approaching from Dr. Callahan's direction.

"Get in the car!"

"What?" Carolina started to turn around.

"Get in the car and get *down!*"

The girls leaped into Flubber's backseat and hit the floorboards, the stinky Ambitien lily flopping down between them.

"This is going great," Kick whispered. "He's going to be way more mad at Dr. Callahan than us and—"

"*Shh!*"

Out in the dusty dirt road, tires crunched closer and this should've made Kick dive closer to the floorboards, but it didn't. *Where's she going? What's she doing?* The questions made Kick peek through the back windows, peering up just enough to see Dr. Callahan's Prius drive past. The psychologist waved at Freeport, and Freeport waved back, smiling like this was any other day.

Which, except for the curse and the Ambitien flower discovery, it would be. Flubber broke down all the time.

"Need any help?" she called.

"No! Thank you, though!" Uncle Freeport laughed. It sounded brittle and breakable as glass. "You know how these things go."

Uncle Freeport can lie really *well under pressure,* Kick thought. He didn't sound like he was talking to a flower-wielding psychopath at *all*.

And Dr. Callahan must have agreed because she drove away.

Kick stuck her head out of Flubber. "She's headed for the town meeting."

"I know." Uncle Freeport had a thick silver hose in his hand. Presumably it was Flubber's. Definitely it was melted. "And she's prepared to subdue the whole town."

Kick tensed. "How do you know that?"

"Because I invented the vaporizer in the backseat of her car."

41

"Or maybe it isn't good luck. I can't tell
if this will be a good thing or a bad thing
for you. Ask me again later."

Uncle Freeport slammed down Flubber's hood and hurled himself into the driver's seat. He cranked the engine once, twice. It growled to life. Smoke streamed from under the hood, and for a second, they couldn't see anything through the windshield.

But then Uncle Freeport stomped on the gas. The smoke thinned, streaming out in all directions. Flubber felt like it was shaking apart underneath them, but Uncle Freeport didn't let up. He powered down the dusty dirt road and into Bohring.

"This is fantastic," Kick told her cousin.

Carolina ignored her. "Dad, how are you going to stop her?"

"The vaporizer will need a few minutes to boil the Ambitien mixture into steam. If I can get to the vaporizer,

I can stop her before the steam hits the crowd. *If* I can get there."

It seemed likely to Kick. She'd never seen her uncle drive so fast. They skidded past the leaning courthouse. They two-wheeled it around the school lane's corner. Dozens and dozens of cars and trucks were parked on either side. At the lane's end, the spiny, spiky schoolyard gate was open, and it looked like the whole town was crowding through.

Freeport slammed on the brakes, double-parking Flubber in front of two red trucks. "Hurry!" he cried, yanking on his seat belt.

Kick and Carolina jumped out of the back, turned for Uncle Freeport—and realized he was still sitting in the driver's seat.

"It's stuck!" Freeport yelled. "I can't get out!" He yanked, yanked, *yanked* on his seat belt, but it wouldn't let go.

Kick gaped. She had no idea what to do. Cut the belt? But with what? Pull on it? Even if both girls pulled as hard as they could, they still weren't as strong as Uncle Freeport, and he couldn't get it loose. That left—

Her uncle swung his head toward them. "Run! Do you understand? I want you to run the other way! If she releases the Ambitien on the crowd—"

The whole town will turn into suggestible zombies, Kick realized. Then Carolina looked at her. They both knew they knew it.

"I can do this," Kick told her.

"What?" her uncle roared. "No, you can't!"

But she could. "It would just take—"

"A vision."

"Karis! Winter!" her uncle yelled, but the girls were already gone. They ran for the spiny, spiky gate, for the crowd that rumbled like distant thunder.

They burst into the schoolyard at a dead run, Kick's eyes scanning all the corners and the edges of the fence. *No vaporizer,* she thought.

And worse: no Dr. Callahan.

She isn't— And then Kick saw her. The blond psychologist was easing toward the school's front steps.

So Kick grabbed Carolina's hand, lowered her head, and launched them into the crowd. They hit the backs of people's knees. They hit the sides of people's legs. Someone swore—actually, a *lot* of someones swore. But Kick held tight to Carolina and bulled her way ahead.

They burst through the last line of legs, and just as Jolene Jones opened her mouth to yell at them, Kick screamed with all her might: "I feel a disturbance in the Force!"

"You kill me, you know that?" Carolina panted, eyes suddenly trained on the ground. "Absolutely kill me. Tone it *down*!"

Kick did not. She spread her arms wide, holding her

hands above her head. "A huge disturbance! This is all a hoax!"

The crowd hissed and drew back a step. "Are you *really* listening to this?" Deputy Patel asked Sheriff Day.

Sheriff Day waved her away. "Hold on. Her grandma's really good at this stuff."

Which made Kick stuff down a grin—and drop both hands to her temples Grandma Missouri–style. "The spirits want us to know we've been tricked! There's a traitor among us!"

"Who's the traitor?" Miss Ruth demanded, but her gaze stayed trained on a sweating Mayor Burr and her eyes were bright like she already knew the answer.

"Dr. Callahan!" Kick pointed a finger at the psychologist and she knew that finger should waver, but she couldn't make herself do it. They had their culprit.

Who was, at that moment, standing at the crowd's edge, her eyes bulging like she was choking down a scream of fury.

"Check her purse!" Kick cried. "Her pockets! Just check . . . *her*!"

"That's way more definitive than I usually get from her grandmother," Miss Cleo murmured to the woman next to her, and the woman murmured something back but Kick never heard it because Sheriff Day practically leaped to Dr. Callahan's side. His eyes wild—*and relieved*, Kick thought—

as he snatched the psychologist's square-shaped handbag from her shoulder.

And pulled out a gas mask.

For a moment, no one breathed a word, and then Dr. Callahan screamed: "How dare you!"

Sheriff Day stared at the gas mask, mouth hanging open. "Why would you have this in your purse?"

Dr. Callahan went pale under her sunburn. "I'm prepared for anything!"

"The spirits say she's lying!" Carolina hollered, and then slapped two hands across her mouth.

"Nice," Kick whispered. "Next time, add how the spirits say she's going to deny it because that's totally coming next."

"Enough," Deputy Patel said, stepping forward so she could grab the gas mask with one hand and Dr. Callahan's arm with the other "Why would you have this?"

"Because she's been poisoning the town with Ambitien powder." It was Uncle Freeport. Everyone turned to watch as he limped into the schoolyard, a swath of seat belt still captured around his waist and a fistful of wires now clasped in his fist. "She was going to poison us again, but I've disabled the vaporizer she was planning to use."

He threw the wires onto the ground. "Ambitien is an invention of mine. It can cause extreme acquiescence."

"An invention of *yours*?" Miss Ruth glowered at Uncle Freeport. "So this is *your* fault?"

"Yes." Uncle Freeport nodded. "It's derived from a plant I developed. I created it to help people, but it quickly got out of hand. I thought by walking away from my job, Ambitien would be done, *over*. I was wrong. I opened the door for someone else to take advantage."

Then he cut Dr. Callahan the strangest look. It should have been filled with fury, but instead Kick saw exhaustion and disappointment warring on his face.

Dr. Callahan lifted her chin. "Scientific advancements don't stop because you think they should, Freeport. When I was hired to replace you, I couldn't *believe* the opportunities you left behind."

"And I can't believe the opportunities you *took*," Freeport countered. "I know you were fired for unethical experiments. Looks like you haven't learned a thing."

"I was recording my findings in Bohring for research!"

"Or to earn your way back to the Larimore Corporation. Admit it, you knew Bohring was the perfect place to test Ambitien because you grew up here. You knew the curse, and you knew there was an opportunity to take advantage."

Dr. Callahan gave him the smallest of smiles, and Kick knew her uncle was right. "And imagine my surprise when I realized you were here," she said, and whipped around, facing the crowd. "Fine! I admit it: I was behind the monsters and the glow and the stench, but I had *nothing* to do with those voices! There's someone else who's playing you too!"

"My dear lady," Mayor Burr began, and everyone's gaze swiveled to him. "No one else is involved in this. Those doorbell sensors came from my store"—a gasp slithered through the crowd—"but I sold them to *you*."

Dr. Callahan went still.

"It's true," the mayor added. "When she first moved here, she ordered dozens of those doorbells. It was odd, but not so odd that I needed to alert the authorities. Until I found out how they had been used."

"He showed me the receipt," Sheriff Day said, stepping away from Kick and Carolina and addressing the crowd. "It was issued two days after she moved to Bohring."

"That's impossible." Dr. Callahan lifted her chin. "Two days after I moved to Bohring, I was waiting at home for propane delivery. Show me my canceled check."

The mayor shrugged. "You paid cash. I only remember it was you because it was such an unusual purchase and I was wise enough to write out a receipt. And propane delivery or not, you still had time to pop into town. I know because I saw you."

"Which means it's your word against hers," Kick announced. She blinked, blinked again. Where had *that* come from?

Then suddenly she knew: Mayor Burr was lying about

something. She could see it in the way he kept swallowing like his mouth was dry, kept darting his gaze around like he was nervous.

Then that gaze landed on Kick.

And something furious zinged through his eyes.

"Your future is . . . hazy. I can't tell if it will be filled with good or bad, but I do know you will have to make a choice."

"That's our Miss Winter." Mayor Burr winked at the crowd. "Always questioning. Thank goodness she's on our side, huh?" Everyone chuckled. "Why don't you come on up here, Miss Winter? Please allow me to *personally* congratulate you on saving our fair town."

He extended his hand, and for the first time, Kick noticed the vans that had pulled up to the schoolyard gates; the people who got out held cameras. In all the excitement, she'd missed them entirely.

But Mayor Burr hadn't.

"You better go," Carolina whispered, nudging Kick forward to join Burr. "Don't embarrass him any further."

Swallowing, Kick climbed up the school's front steps. The mayor threw one arm around her shoulders, angling them around to face the cameras as he shook her hand. The whole town was watching them. Kick could see everyone from Mrs. Flagg (looking proud) to the Jennas (looking disgusted) to Dr. Hazmat (still looking befuddled).

"Smile for us, Miss Winter," the mayor boomed as the cameras flashed. "We're all so proud of you!"

It was almost exactly like she'd dreamed—then Burr leaned in close. "You don't have a *thing* to prove my involvement," he breathed, still smiling, still shaking her hand. "But you do have *everything* to lose. Let it go."

"So you *were* behind the doorbell sensors," Kick whispered.

"It was going to make me look in control."

"And then *we* happened."

"Everything to lose, Kick Winter." Mayor Burr straightened, patted her on the shoulder like they were the best of friends, and applauded as he sent her back down the steps. "What a great example of what Bohring residents are capable of."

True, Kick thought, suddenly chilled. But now *she* knew what Bohring mayors were capable of.

Burr turned back to the crowd, hand over his heart.

And his Vote for Burr button.

"My friends," he said, "I made a horrible mistake by trusting this outsider, but it won't happen ever again! And remember, I went to the authorities as soon as I figured out what was going on."

"We're so lucky to have a mayor with such foresight." Sheriff Day began to clap, and after a few seconds of hesitation, the townspeople began to clap too.

Mayor Burr ducked his head. "And we're also lucky to have such an amazing sheriff and deputy."

The clapping increased. One of the reporters forced her way through the crowd. "I'm Liv St. Boar," she said, thrusting a black microphone toward the two men, "I'm with the *Atlanta Journal-Constitution*. Mayor Burr, your town was almost poisoned. Could this happen again?"

"Let's go," Uncle Freeport said quietly.

"But shouldn't you stay?" Carolina asked as they followed him toward Flubber. "They should be asking *you* about Ambitien, not the mayor."

Her father rubbed one hand over his jaw, considering the question. There were shadows under his eyes.

Behind his eyes.

He looked at Kick. "Did Burr say something to you?"

"You don't understand!" Dr. Callahan shrieked behind them. Deputy Patel was steering her toward the waiting police cruiser—or trying to steer her. Callahan dug her pointy heels into the dirt and refused to budge. "The only job I could get after being fired was *here*! As a school *psychologist*! What would you have done?"

"Not this!" Deputy Patel yanked on Dr. Callahan, and Dr. Callahan yanked back.

"I had nothing to do with those voices!" she screamed.

Everyone winced. Well, everyone except for Uncle Freeport. When they reached the spiny, spiky schoolyard gate, he stopped, turned. "Kick? *Did* he say something to you?"

"Yeah," she finally managed. "He admitted he was behind the voices. He lied when he said Dr. Callahan bought everything from him. *He* rigged the doorbell sensors to create a problem he could fix. He wanted reelection."

Usually knowledge made Kick feel better.

But right now, it made her feel so much worse.

"I'm telling you, someone else is behind the voices!" Dr. Callahan dug her heels in harder, and Sheriff Day had to come help Deputy Patel. They each grabbed an arm as she thrashed. "You don't understand! I was doing this for *good*!"

"Enough of that!" Sheriff Day shouted.

"But I *was*. It was going to be wonderful—the advancements would have changed the way we do things, the way we understand things."

And put like that? It sounded noble. Noble enough that Kick hesitated. Noble enough that she saw a little of herself in Dr. Callahan—maybe more than a little. Discovering things had always felt right to her. She wondered if it had always felt right to Dr. Callahan too. If the whole thing started out very differently than how it ended up.

And suddenly Kick thought she might know the *why*

after all. The swamp was just a swamp until someone needed it to be more—just like science was science, until someone wanted to use it. Dr. Callahan wanted answers, and she wanted those answers so much she was willing to use anyone to get to them.

"So he's going to get away with it?" Carolina asked, voice soft. "They aren't even going to question him?"

Mayor Burr was still talking to the reporters. He was smiling and joking, and the reporters were smiling and joking. No one suspected a thing.

He looked like a hero.

"C'mon," Uncle Freeport said, leading the girls deeper into the darkening street. Night was coming, and the air was already beginning to smell like water. "Admitting it to Kick isn't enough proof to arrest him. Sometimes justice takes time."

"I thought it was supposed to be swift," Carolina grumbled.

"Not for everyone." And there was something Kick didn't understand in her uncle's tone, something sad and resigned.

He expected this, Kick realized, but she didn't understand why.

"I'm so proud of you two," Uncle Freeport added, a small smile touching the corners of his mouth as he opened Flubber's rear door for them. "You were just like movie detectives. You figured out everything we couldn't see."

Kick smiled back, but the smile didn't fit. She wasn't like a detective in a movie at all. At the end of a movie, everyone was happy and relieved—and while it did seem like everyone in Bohring was indeed happier and more relieved, solving the mystery had raised more questions than it had answered.

Questions like, why would Dr. Callahan do something like this? Why would Mayor Burr do something like this? Why did the people of Bohring matter so little to them?

Why?

Kick slid across Flubber's backseat, Carolina joining her. Grandma Missouri was right. *Why* really was the most important question, and it *was* the one nobody ever asked. It was the one nobody answered either.

Uncle Freeport climbed in the (a bit mangled) driver's seat and turned to the girls. "I wish you had come to me sooner."

"I know," Kick said. "I'm sorry."

"I'm sorry too. Maybe instead of just keeping you and Carolina out of it all, I should have told you *why* I wanted you out of it. I made a mistake. I underestimated you."

Kick perked up. "Does this mean we're not grounded?"

Uncle Freeport laughed and laughed. "Oh, no. You're grounded."

She frowned—though technically speaking, she understood. "Honestly, Uncle Freeport, by the time I was in it, I couldn't get out—not without making things worse."

Her uncle nodded, turning his key in the ignition and trying to urge Flubber back to life. "You're never so deep into a lie that you can't come clean, *if* you're brave enough. Do you know why I really left the Larimore Corporation?"

The cousins exchanged a glance and then shook their heads. "No, why?" Kick asked.

"Because it's never too late to be the person you want to be. I hope you will grow up to live a life you're proud of, and if you're not? I hope you both will have the courage to change."

Carolina nodded, and after a beat, so did Kick. She hadn't been so good at changing, but maybe she could do better.

Beneath them, Flubber roared to life, and Uncle Freeport patted the dash. "And just to show you what I mean, I'm going to make a change right now. Keeping you two out of my laboratory? Not anymore. I'm not going to hide my discoveries from you anymore. I'm going to make sure you know what to do with them—and no more walking away. By doing nothing, I let this happen. From now on, I'm going to fight back. I'm going to speak *up*."

Kick studied her uncle, and though he looked as he always looked—albeit a good deal more tired and worn— he seemed different as well. She could see the scientist in him, the man who had walked away from everything he'd wanted, the man who was going to be something more.

I wonder what people see when they look at me, she thought. Maybe that didn't matter nearly as much as what she saw when she looked at herself. And then it hit her: Instead of focusing on getting kids who would never like her for who she was, she needed to focus on kids who would like her for *exactly* who she was.

Maybe I should start a science club, Kick thought. *All my family helps people in different ways. Maybe teaching people about science could be mine? Maybe . . . Maybe I'm more like them than I thought? Yeah, I'm going to be a world-famous scientist, but I could be a world-famous scientist who helps kids like me* also *become world-famous scientists.*

Carolina sighed. "Who would've thought this could happen in Bohring?"

"No one," Kick said.

"At least it's over."

She snatched a glance at her cousin. Was that *regret* in Carolina's tone? Was she disappointed the adventure was done?

"It'll never be over," Uncle Freeport said, and there was *definitely* regret in his tone. "As long as knowledge can be used for power, people will seek it out, and now that Miss St. Boar is going to tell the world what's happened . . .

well . . . Bohring needs to brace itself. We're about to get a lot more attention."

Kick frowned. Put like that it sounded horribly scary (since Uncle Freeport seemed so worried) and yet also delightfully interesting (because obviously). "What kind of attention?"

"That remains to be seen." Again, there was that grim note stamped into Uncle Freeport's voice.

And everyone thinks Grandma Missouri's the dramatic one. "Well, whatever's coming, we'll be ready," Kick said. She gave him her winningest smile and was it her imagination or did Uncle Freeport smile back just a little bit? He *did*! "But if we're about to get overrun with tourists or reporters, I'm guessing you're going to need to upgrade the security around your laboratory. Like, *way* upgrade it."

"I agree."

"Oh, good! Because I have a few ideas about security systems." Kick felt her grin stretch wide. Wider. "How do you feel about explosives?"

The
Experiments
of
KICK WINTER

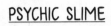

PSYCHIC SLIME

USE

General awesomeness

SUPPLIES

- 1 cup hot tap water (But not *too* hot. Or use hazmat suit. Note to self: Get hazmat suit.)
- 4 ounces clear liquid glue (Use non-toxic in case Butler tries to eat it. Again.)
- 3 tablespoons glow-in-the-dark craft paint
- 2 teaspoons Borax
- 1 big bowl (Check Grandma Missouri's cupboard.)
- 1/3 cup hot tap water (but not *too* hot) in small, separate bowl

STEPS

1. Pour hot water into the big bowl.
2. Add glue.
3. Add glow-in-the-dark paint. Stir everything together.
4. Add Borax to small bowl of hot water. Stir.
5. ~~Dump Borax water into glue mixture.~~
6. SLOWLY pour Borax water into glue mixture.
7. Try a spoonful at a time. Keep stirring.
8. Turn off lights. EEK!

Runny slime needs less Borax!

SWAMP HOLLOW GAS

USE
Room de-freshener; friend repellent

SUPPLIES
I large garlic clove (or an onion)
I small bowl
Rubbing alcohol
Dish soap
5 tablespoons water (leftover water from steamed broccoli
or brussels sprouts is even better)
Bubble wand

STEPS
1. Chop garlic into small pieces.
2. Press garlic pieces with the back of a spoon to squeeze out juice.
3. Pour garlic bits and juice into small bowl.
4. Add 1 teaspoon of rubbing alcohol. Stir.
5. Cover bowl and let sit for 15 minutes (or longer for smellier).
6. Add 1 tablespoon of dish soap to garlic-alcohol mixture.
7. Add 5 tablespoons of water.
8. Stir gently. *Really* gently. Avoid suds!
9. Dip bubble wand into mixture and blow. *POOF!* Swamp bubbles!

THE SILENT SOUND EFFECT

USE

Not sure yet. Private concert, maybe?

SUPPLIES

I wire coat hanger (or small metal baking rack,
   or metal whisk)
2 pieces of yarn or string, 2 to 3 feet long
   (Check Grandma Missouri's knitting supplies.)
Wall

STEPS

1. Tightly knot one end of each piece of yarn to opposite
   sides of metal object.
2. Twirl the loose end of one piece of yarn around tip of
   right index finger, 10 loops; twirl the loose end of the other
   piece of yarn around left index finger, 10 loops.
3. Place twirled yarn (on fingers) against the outside of each
   ear canal. (Right finger to the right ear; left finger to the
   left ear.) Don't poke inside of ears!
4. Keep yarn-wrapped fingers against ears; swing object
   against wall.
5. Listen! *BOING!*

BOING

EYE SLEIGHT

USE

Confusing enemies? Secret directions to laboratory?

SUPPLIES

Large clear glass

Water

Arrow (drawn, no wider than the glass)

STEPS

1. Fill glass with water.
2. Position the arrow behind the glass, several inches away.
3. Look through the front of the glass.
4. WHAT?! Switcheroo!

MRS. FLAGG'S CABBAGE CLONES

USE
None at present. Nobody likes cabbage. *But* good practice for future cloning work.

SUPPLIES
- 1 cabbage
- 3 paper towel sheets
- 3 resealable plastic bags

STEPS
1. Pull off all the cabbage leaves. Make coleslaw (optional).
2. Keep the stem.
3. Cut the stem into three even slices. (Ask Grandma Missouri for help. Tell her it's for school.)
4. Separate the three pieces: top of stem, middle of stem, bottom of stem.
5. Label plastic bags: TOP, MIDDLE, BOTTOM.
6. Place the matching stem piece into each bag.
7. Fold three paper towels in fourths. Lightly dampen each one.
8. Place one paper towel into each bag.
9. Stuff each cabbage stem inside the middle of the paper towel. (It looks like a cabbage sandwich. Ew.)
10. Blow a small amount of air into the first bag. Seal it shut. Repeat for each bag.
11. Place bags near a window. (Make sure Butler can't find them. Or Grandma Missouri.)
12. Once a day, open the bag and record observations until—AHH!—creepy cabbage clones start growing.

TRICK LIQUID SAND

USE
Because obviously. Trick. Liquid. Sand.

SUPPLIES
 One scientist, engineer, or handy adult
 PVC pipes, elbows, tees
 PVC pipe glue
 Extra fitting pieces
 Big plastic container
 Drill
 Drill bits
 Superfine sand
 Air compressor

STEPS
1. Research "fluidized liquid sand." Find instructions.
2. Gather scientist, engineer, or handy adult.
3. Show scientist, engineer, or handy adult research and instructions.
4. Beg scientist, engineer, or handy adult to help try the experiment.
5. If step 4 fails, repeat steps 1-4 with another scientist, engineer, or handy adult.
6. If step 5 fails, wow friends and relatives with liquid sand facts instead.

ACKNOWLEDGMENTS

It's weird to see *The Monster Hypothesis* with only my name on it because, goodness knows, I didn't get here on my own. I'm beyond grateful to everyone who helped me—and there were so many people.

So *very* many.

In no particular order, huge thanks to my parents (as always) for being so supportive. You saw Kick years ago and knew she was special. Thank you for encouraging me to stick with her.

Similarly, thank you to Wonder Agent, Sarah Davies, who *also* saw Kick years ago and believed in her.

But Kick wouldn't even be, well, *Kick* without my long-suffering editors, Tracey Keevan and Esther Cajahuaringa. Thank you for helping me make her everything she needed to be. It's a better book because of you. I'm a better writer because of you.

Special thanks also to Maggie Coughlin for . . . everything. You put me back together when I was trying my best to spin apart. I'm incredibly lucky to have you in my life. Incredibly.

More special thanks to Tae Keller for your fantastic insights. I will forever be your biggest fangirl.

All the thank-yous to Natalie Richards and Pintip Dunn for your early reads . . . and later reads . . . and then *later* reads. Thank you for seeing me at my rawest and letting me make mistakes.

And, of course, thanks to Mark Rober for experiment permissions and inspiration. I watched your YouTube channel for ages before daring to follow along.

But "following along" wouldn't have even been possible without Jennifer Zitt, teacher/science consultant extraordinaire. Thank you for helping me pull everything together. I'm quite sure I sounded ridiculous during our calls. I apologize.

Above all, though, I want to thank my beta readers—some of whom would prefer not to be named even though I would shout their brilliance from the rooftops—you are extraordinary women and I am forever grateful you read for me. Special, *special* thanks to Athena Higgins and Gina Hill for last-minute reads and honest insights. What a hairy weekend. Thank you. Without y'all I would *never* have pulled it off.